KU-270-268

A CASE OF ART FAILURE

Two London typists see an advertisement for a painting seminar in the country and decide that it would be a novel way to spend their vacation. The school is for advanced students only and they know nothing about art, but they hope to conceal that fact and to learn how to paint. What they do not expect are the accidents and violent deaths which occur. Is someone trying to eliminate them one by one?

REDCAR AND CLEVELAND

WITHDRAWN

LIBRARIES

Books by Freda Bream
in the Linford Mystery Library:

ISLAND OF FEAR
THE VICAR INVESTIGATES
WITH MURDER IN MIND
THE CORPSE ON THE CRUISE
MURDER IN THE MAP ROOM
THE VICAR DONE IT
COFFIN TO LET

FREDA BREAM

A CASE OF ART FAILURE

Complete and Unabridged

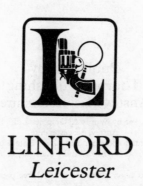

LINFORD
Leicester

First published in Great Britain

First Linford Edition
published December 1994

Copyright © 1984 by Freda Bream
All rights reserved

British Library CIP Data

Bream, Freda
    A case of art failure.—Large print ed.—
Linford mystery library
I. Title II. Series
823 [F]

ISBN 0–7089–7636–0

Published by
F. A. Thorpe (Publishing) Ltd.
Anstey, Leicestershire

Set by Words & Graphics Ltd.
Anstey, Leicestershire
Printed and bound in Great Britain by
T. J. Press (Padstow) Ltd., Padstow, Cornwall

This book is printed on acid-free paper

1

IT was Ralph Hopkins, the relieving records clerk, who really started the whole affair. Relieving clerks, those seemingly negligible, transitory beings, have yet a tendency to upset the placid routine of an old-established firm. They break in fresh and beaming from the outside world, skip through the office premises for a fortnight, then take their pay and depart, unaware of the changes they may have wrought in the lives of those they leave behind.

You might say it was not the man Hopkins' fault, for he was merely voicing an opinion. Carr and Dawson, Public Accountants, encouraged their employees to voice opinions. The utterance of personal views has a healthy cathartic effect on the attitude to work, Mr Dawson used to say. Mr Carr concurred. And as neither partner let himself in any way be influenced by the staff's opinions, he was fully in favour of their expression, providing that it took place during a tea-break and not in working hours.

On this particular morning, the relieving clerk Hopkins was standing in the typists' room, holding a sugared bun in one hand and a mug of lukewarm coffee in the other. His face was flushed with animation, as he spoke with the vigour and confidence of the normal healthy young man who has a message for mankind. He waved his bun at intervals to give emphasis to his words. "It's a masterful and meaningful work of art, executed by one not tamely adhering to rigid traditional values. You condemn it because you have insufficient knowledge to appreciate its underlying significance or the competence of the technique."

Carol Barton, the senior typist, gave what in a less attractive young female could be called a snort. "Rot!" she said bluntly. "*Emotion 25*! Even the title's loopy."

"You don't *understand*," moaned Ralph.

"Why should I have to? Art isn't just for a closed circle of people who have studied it. You don't need to take a cordon bleu course before you can enjoy a rump steak, or do an apprenticeship in tailoring if you want to buy a suit. *Emotion 25*! What utter nonsense! Don't you think so, Susan?"

Susan Meadows, Carol's close friend, had been listening quietly. Now she nodded. "Ralph thinks we don't know much because we're only typists and didn't go to University or Art School. But we know what we like, Ralph, and we do not like that — that *Thing*."

"*Thing's* the word for it," said Carol. "You can't call it a picture. It's just an appalling splotch which some scoundrel conned poor Mr Carr into buying. To present that *Thing* to poor old Mr Murchison on his retirement is enough to induce galloping senility."

"On the contrary," said Ralph Hopkins severely, "he'll be in possession of a fine example of abstract art, one which will increase in value with the years. Mr Carr showed excellent taste. Look at it! Depth — feeling — notice how the distortion of the white circle emphasises the linear strength of the interlocking red and orange squares."

"Huh! I think a kid did it with one hand while he was watching telly. Three lopsided squares, half a circle, and a few daubs of colour which don't even look good together. Anyone could do that. *I* could do it. There's no skill needed. What you call abstract art is one of the biggest commercial swindles of modern times."

Ralph regarded her sadly. She *looked* intelligent enough, which just proved that one can never tell. With a cramped mentality like that, she would probably burst into tears if she were given a round sandwich instead of a triangular one — clinging to the standards she had meekly accepted in her childhood — moving in a cosy little padded nest like a white mouse, and with about the same amount of independent thought. "It's no use arguing with you," he said resignedly. "Until you know more about art and have broader vision it's a waste of time. I merely assure you that with knowledge comes understanding, with understanding appreciation, with greater appreciation comes — "

"Mr Dawson," said the cashier. "Back to work, all. Time's up."

Emotion 25 was two days later handed over to the departing Mr Murchison at a formal little ceremony attended by all the staff. He thanked the assembled company for the — er — unusual — work of art. Then he placed it under his brief-case while he ate his ration of savouries and cream sponge, and was later seen stowing it in the boot of his car with a wondering, bewildered expression as he did so. "It's the bleak prospect of retirement," said Mr Carr, as he watched from a window.

"Empty years ahead, and the task of fulfilling them fruitfully." Mr Dawson agreed.

On Friday afternoon Ralph Hopkins made brief farewells to the Carr and Dawson employees, and then walked into the street, out of their lives.

One morning in the following week Carol Barton suddenly stopped typing and looked purposefully across at Susan Meadows. She had something to say, and for some time had been nerving herself to say it. So much depended on Susan's reaction. She ran her fingers thoughtfully through her dark, curly hair, and then said tentatively, "He *could* be right, you know, Susan."

Susan looked up. "If it's one of Mr Dawson's letters, he isn't. He never is. Spell it your own way."

"Not him. That relieving guy — you know, Ralph."

"What about him?"

"Like I said. He could be right. What he said about art. We don't know anything about it really, do we?

6

We've never done any."

"I wove a cane tray once when I was in the fourth form at St Margaret's. The teacher said it was *very* good, and they put it in the end of year exhibition of pupils' work."

"That doesn't help you understand modern art. I've been thinking."

"Well?"

"Well, take bricklaying."

"I'd hate to. What are you talking about?"

"It's so easy to lay bricks. All you do is plonk one down, spread some sticky muck on top, then slap on another. Simple. Yet the apprenticeship period is five years. Why? There must be something I've overlooked."

"Yes, you need a spirit-level and a plumb-bob."

"Five years should teach you more than that. See what I mean? So perhaps we were a bit hasty about that picture, *Emotion 25*. It may have had something we missed out on. Take thatching roofs. The apprenticeship period is seven years, isn't it? Yet all you have to do is grab a bundle of dried grass and — "

"Don't explain. I get the idea."

"If we painted, ourselves, we'd see the difficulties and what the artist was trying to achieve and maybe we'd have liked the *Thing* a bit better. We should have examined it more closely and with a more open mind."

"Too late now. Poor old Mr Murchison is stuck with it. A darned shame. A nice old codger like that. I bet his wife stuck it in the attic."

"It's not too late for us to find out why Ralph liked it."

"What do you mean? Oh, Carol, you have that glint in your eye. What are you up to now?" Susan looked over at the eager face and lively brown eyes of her friend. "Come on, out with it."

Carol leaned forward, then spoke slowly, trying to curb her enthusiasm. "You said you were doing nothing special in the holidays, now that Jim's gone to Spain. I saw an ad in the

Telegraph last night." She pulled open the top drawer of her desk, brought out her handbag and opened it. "Here it is." She handed over a small newspaper cutting and anxiously watched Susan's face as she read it. If only she would consent! It was in her own interests to do so. She'd mope if she stayed at home.

Susan was reading the cutting, frowning slightly. But then she nearly always looked serious. That smooth pearly skin, the long straight fair hair, and those wide, earnest blue eyes — oh, that idiot Jim! He had been so inattentive lately, and Carol knew, as Susan must surely know, that had he wished he could easily have postponed his business trip to Spain until after Susan's annual vacation. The backsliding worm!

"Well, what do you think, Sue?"

"Hm — *park-like surroundings — good cuisine — expert tuition — owing to cancellations, a few vacancies now available for the August 4th session*. I don't believe that bit. That's a sales gimmick. *Tutors include the well-known Jane Pillington*. I've never heard of her."

"That just shows how ignorant we are. What about it, Sue? It fits in so well. The firm closes for three weeks on 1st August, and this starts on the 4th."

Susan's lips twitched. "It's tempting, isn't it? It would be something different. But it says *advanced tuition for artists*. They wouldn't take us."

"They needn't know we're not artists."

"They'd soon find out."

"Then it would be too late to chuck us out. Anyway, who says we're not artists? You wove a cane tray once, and I used to draw mice for the next-door neighbour's little boy. Round mice with long tails. Oh, think of all we'd learn, Sue!"

"It's awfully expensive."

"It's cheaper than going to Majorca."

"But we weren't going to Majorca."

"That doesn't alter the fact that it's

cheaper than going there if we were," Carol pointed out. "Or weren't," she added fairly.

"It's out of the question. We can't pretend to be artists."

"Yes, we can. I've had an idea about that. We could say that we want to specialise in a branch of art we have previously neglected. How's that? Then we wouldn't be expected to know anything about it."

"The branches we've neglected will give us wide scope," smiled Susan. "But we haven't even — "

"We can buy them. Just a few paints and some paper and brushes."

"But how would — "

"We'd go in my car."

"I'm not sure if I — "

"I can lend you some."

"But — "

"Susan, don't be cross, will you? *Please* don't be cross. I rang them up last night. There were just two vacancies, so I booked us in."

2

"I LOVE these Sussex lanes," said Carol happily. The late afternoon sun was still warm, the car was running smoothly, and she had a feeling of well-being which made her brown eyes sparkle.

"They'll find us out," said Susan gloomily. She was staring at the road ahead, half regretting that she had allowed Carol's enthusiasm and persuasive powers to inveigle her into this particular way of spending her three weeks' annual holiday. "*Advanced tuition*, it said. For artists. And we can't even draw. *Highly qualified tutors*, it said. All the other students will be real, experienced artists."

Carol secretly hoped that the other students would be young, healthy, unattached males, to form a selection from which Susan could choose a substitute for her ex-admirer Jim. Sue's despondency was more likely due to his defection than anything else. The rotter. He didn't know what he was turning down. Susan mightn't be a beauty queen. A small slender figure, straight blonde hair, a serious expression — plain, perhaps, until she smiled, and then her whole face lit up. And she was a *good* person, sincere, affectionate, always thinking of others. Why had that stupid fool cooled off? Susan was well rid of him, but the trouble was she didn't know it yet.

"*Highly qualified*, it said," repeated Susan. "For *advanced tuition*."

"The better qualified they are, the more they'll be able to teach us," Carol pointed out. "I wonder if we should tell them straight away that we've never done any art? No, that might prejudice them against us. Better as we planned — we've specialised and now want to extend our fields. You've done only black and white, and you want to try abstract, which is why you bought pastels."

"You know darned well I bought pastels because they were the cheapest materials in the shop."

"You chose pastels because you've never worked with them before, and you considered they would be suitable for abstract art."

Susan smiled. "If you like." Carol's bubbling effervescence made her feel old sometimes, even though she was in reality four years younger. She was twenty-seven now, and Carol thirty-one. Gosh, they were both old. Spinsters on the shelf. She was old and plain and dull. Jim could hardly be blamed for going off to look for something younger and more attractive. Carol, though — Carol would be charming for years yet. She had that sort of face. It was a constant source of surprise to Susan that her friend had never married.

"You'll be safe," Carol was saying. "If they criticise your efforts just

14

say they don't grasp the underlying significance."

"What about you? Why did you buy water colours?"

"Because you got in first with the pastels, and oils are too expensive. But I'll let them think that I've done oils and now wish to try landscape painting in watercolour."

"They'll swallow that?"

"It doesn't matter whether they do or not. The director is more likely to be a grasping business man than an evangelist for the fine arts. He just wants our fees. And they can't turn us out, because we've paid."

"A *concentrated course*. We'll be fed, won't we?"

"That's the not the right attitude, girl. Artists don't eat. But the ad said *good cuisine*. Look, I think we're almost there. Where are those instructions?" She pulled up and took a sheet of paper from the glove-box. "*Approximately three miles past the village of Little Dorley, turn left at the Vintner's Head* — we did that — *over a small bridge* — that's it ahead — *continue for one mile and from the top of the rise the gateposts will be clearly visible*. Off we go then. Here's the bridge. This is quite a hill, not a mere rise — oh, so they *are* visible! That's it, Sue. On the right there. Look."

She slowed the car, and they were left in no doubt, for a large notice over a stone gate-post informed them *Flavell Art Institute. Summer School. John P. Flavell, director*. The large iron gates were open, revealing extensive grounds. Carol drove slowly along an avenue of huge old chestnut trees. The sun made dappled patches in the shadow of their leaves.

"They weren't fooling," said Susan. "It is a park. It's smashing. Do you think we'll have to paint these trees? Trees must be awfully difficult."

"Not for you. You'll do them all as yellow and purple squares."

The drive curved round to the right,

rising slightly, and the house came into view. It was an imposing building of mellowed, ivy-covered stone, with two main storeys and attic rooms above. The ground fell away on the left, showing distant fields, misty hills and the glimpse of a lake glittering in the late sunlight. Carol parked her car alongside others on a paved area, and they carried their cases across to the wide shallow steps. On each side of the top one was a large carved stone animal. "These aren't the usual griffins," remarked Susan. "They're cheetahs or panthers, aren't they? Or leopards, maybe? They remind me of something I've seen before."

The door was opened to them by a plumpish middle-aged woman with a pleasant face. "You're Misses Barton and Meadows? I'm the housekeeper here. My name is Ballins. Do come in." She took their cases from them.

The reception hall was spacious, lined with oak panelling. Several doors and a passage opened off it, and a broad staircase curved gracefully from the centre to the right. On the walls were hung portraits, painted in oils now darkened with age, and held in old, carved, wooden frames.

Susan looked around in awe. "Isn't it a shame to use such a lovely old building for a school?"

"It's the family home of Mrs Flavell. All new students admire it."

"Is that why they give art lessons? For the maintenance of the house and the grounds? It must cost a lot."

"Oh no," said the housekeeper. "There's money enough in the Estate, and Mrs Flavell has private means from other sources too. They don't need to teach at all. They just want to pass on their knowledge. That is — at least — Mr Flavell. Come, I'll show you to your rooms."

She walked purposefully to the stairs, and Carol had the impression that she felt she had said too much. If the Flavells had adequate income, and taught only for the love of art, why did they charge such high fees for doing so? Was it to exclude the riff-raff, those who would be out of place in this old ancestral home, or who would not respect its valuable contents? "How many students are there?" she asked, as they followed Mrs Ballins up to the first landing.

"You're the sixth and seventh to arrive. There's Miss Satterley still to come. Mr Flavell takes only eight at a time, you know. It's a highly concentrated course, with individual tuition."

"Are there many tutors?"

"Only Mr Flavell and his wife, and this year Miss Pillington. *Jane* Pillington, you know. *The* Jane Pillington. They're lucky to have her. Oh, you'll enjoy it. Everyone does. But you both look so young."

"Are most of the students old?"

"Older than you, but we get all ages. There are four sessions each summer, you see, three weeks each. And it's so popular. The very best artists come, even ones who are hung in the Tate or the National."

"Oh, *do* they?" gasped Susan. "Are they *all* terribly good?"

"They're all excellent artists, but even in the best here are gaps of knowledge and experience, that's what Mr Flavell says. They help one another too. He says there's always something to learn, and that's the benefit of a course like this."

"Oh, help!" moaned Susan. She looked so appalled that Carol changed the subject.

"Do you live here all the time, Mrs Ballins?"

"My husband and I have been here about eighteen months now."

"Do you like it?"

"Yes, it's a good job. There's no more staff, except for a jobbing gardener at times and a woman who comes in to clean the windows and the silver. We work three weeks without a break and then have seven or eight days off between sessions. And the students are mostly very considerate, like making their own beds." She looked hopefully at them each in turn, a question in her eye.

"Of course we shall too," Carol assured her. "That's no trouble."

"Oh, thank you, dear. And last winter, when there were no teaching sessions, we were kept on full pay, even though there was nothing much to do, because Mrs Flavell went to stay with relatives, and Mr Flavell was out most of the day, all weathers. I tell him he'll catch his death, but he gets so many commissions, you see. He enjoys it, too. A real artist, and *such* a nice gentleman. Here you are. You have connecting rooms with a bathroom in between. Dinner will be in about an hour's time, but there's no formality here, so you needn't bother to change unless you want to. Some do, some don't. It's a working party, you know, not a social gathering, that's what Mr Flavell says. When you've freshened up come on down and I'll introduce you to the others." She smiled and left them.

The bedrooms were small, obviously partitioned out of larger rooms, but all was clean and fresh. The beds were firm. In each room was an easy-chair, but also a table and stool, indicating that one was expected to work at night. A small dresser held tea-making materials. From each window could be seen fertile valleys, tall trees, and distant hills bathed in a soft, misty light.

"It's heavenly," breathed Carol. "So peaceful. Even if we don't learn to paint, it's a lovely place for a holiday. Let's hurry. I'm anxious to meet the others. You can go first with the bathroom."

Mrs Ballins was waiting for them when they went downstairs. With a smile she opened the door to a large sitting-room. "We call this the common-room. It used to be the morning-room, but Mr Flavell says the term is out of place now."

It was a large, elegantly proportioned

room, giving a first impression to Carol of a haphazard mixture of old and new. It seemed that no interest had been taken in preserving the character or history of the house. A few period pieces had been retained, but the modern furniture had not been chosen to harmonise with them, and the carpet and curtains were incongruously of bold, harsh design. It was not the way she would have furnished it, thought Carol, but then she was not an artist. The owners must know best. She'd think about it later. At present she was more interested in the five people in the room, who had turned to look at her and Susan.

"Miss Barton and Miss Meadows," announced Mrs Ballins. "I'll introduce you each in turn, so please carry on with what you're doing."

She led them first to a tall, muscular woman standing by the window, with feet astride and arms folded. She had short, straight brown hair, a long face and strong features. She was dressed in grey slacks and a green shirt, and wore no make-up. "Miss Myra Hurst," said Miss Ballins.

The woman nodded, and in a gruff manly voice in keeping with her appearance said, "Hope you'll like it here." Then having fulfilled her social obligations, she turned back to look out of the window again.

"Mr Sullivan." A small, thin, elderly man rose courteously from his chair and held out a gnarled hand. "Delighted to meet you. I hope you'll enjoy your stay as much as I intend to do." His hair was white but still thick. His blue eyes were shrewd and bright. Carol liked him at once.

They moved on to a group of three. One was a woman in her sixties, listening smilingly to two men who were having a heated discussion. "But if you're aiming at an ideal of organic harmony, it is questionable whether the merit of visual immediacy — "

"Miss Tritt," said Mrs Ballins, and the woman turned to greet them. She

24

was somewhat like the housekeeper herself. A little plumper, a little older, but with the same benevolent expression and placid smile. She had grey hair, untidily pinned up, and wore thick-lensed spectacles, the sort of woman you would less expect to find attending an advanced course in the fine arts than to be sitting in an easy-chair in a Brighton boarding-house, knitting for her great-nephews.

"Eva Tritt," she told them. "Just call me Eva. I'm so pleased to meet you."

The men were introduced as Rudolph Stein and Vance Mackay. Stein was a stocky, solid man in his early thirties, with thick, short fair hair, a square face, and a square beard, which accentuated his aggressive chin. Carol appraised him briefly and decided he was not the type for Susan. He would bully her. The other was more promising, a tall, lean man whose age she also put in the thirties. He had no beard or moustache, but his hair was too long for her taste. Long hair was on the way out, didn't he know that? Yet it was well groomed — clothes a bit sloppy — that pullover had seen better days — a sensitive face, good eyes, intellectual brow. Yes, he'd do for starters.

"Don't you agree, Miss Barton?" The stocky one, Stein, was looking at her keenly, and she realised that lost in her assessment of them both for her own purposes she had failed to follow the conversation.

"Perhaps," she said wisely, and Mr Stein gave her a rather amused look as he nodded.

"On the other hand," he went on, "it might be said that Claes Oldenburg is presenting what he considers a legible image of an essential truth." The look he gave her was hard and measuring.

"Undoubtedly," agreed Carol, "that *could* be said." She was not going to be intimidated by those piercing eyes.

"Now, you two, come along and tell me all about yourselves," said Miss Tritt. She took them to a group of easy-chairs. "I was glad to get away," she said as she sat down. "It's interesting to hear them talk, but I don't really understand what they say. I'm not a good artist, you see. They don't serve sherry the first night. I really don't know why. It's just the first night you need it most, don't you think? You're new to the course, aren't you? Or have you been before?"

"No, we haven't," said Susan. "Have you? And the others?"

Miss Tritt leaned forward and told them proudly, "I've been for the last *four years*. But I'm not an artist, like all you people. You see, they took beginners when I started, so I was lucky, and they've let me come back. Isn't that *kind*? I'm the only one not a real artist, but I do enjoy it. They're always so nice to me. I never did any art until I retired. I was in a shop, you know, the Fuller Figure boutique in Ashford, and we paid into a pension fund, though I sometimes think I should have taken up weaving instead."

"Have the others been before?"

"Myra Hurst comes at the same time as I do every year. That's the tall lady in slacks by the window over there. She's ever so good. She's in the Girdpark gallery, you know. Like Mr Sullivan. Isn't he a sweet old gentleman? So polite always. And gifted, Myra says. He's in line for the Sanderson-Ebbings award, I believe, like Myra. But it's his first time here, Myra says. It makes you wonder why they come, doesn't it? When they're so good themselves, I mean. You wouldn't think they'd have anything to learn, would you? Not like me. It was so nice of them to let me keep on when they changed the course to an advanced one. Mr Flavell's very kind about it, so helpful, you know, and I *am* making progress, I really am. He says so. And Myra helps me too. She doesn't seem to mind and yet she's so clever herself."

"What about the others?" asked Susan as Miss Tritt momentarily stopped for breath.

"I've never seen them before and I think they're new. Mind you, I can't say for certain. There are four sessions each summer, you see. But Myra Hurst says they're new, and she would know. Of course, I've heard of Mr Stein and seen photos of his *Woman with Spoon*. That's his best, they say. You wouldn't think he'd be asking for help. But Myra says it's the stimulation to work that he must come for, like herself. I'm sure I don't know. What do you think? In my opinion, it shows a nice attitude. Not stuck-up, if you know what I mean. Like Myra too. Though sculpting isn't quite the same, is it? Perhaps he doesn't paint very well. Where do you live? Oh, my *cousin* flatted in Putney — "

She chattered on volubly, but there was something so happy and artless about her twittering, and it was so patently without malice or envy, that when she asked, "What do you two do? Should I know your names? Are you very famous?" a sudden impulse prompted Carol to blurt out, "We're not artists. We haven't done any art at all, but we didn't say so when we applied to come, because we thought they might turn us down. Do you think they'll find out? And will they mind?"

Miss Tritt's eyes widened, and she stared in a brief silence. Then she burst out laughing, throwing her head back and chuckling merrily. "Well, what do you know! How brave of you to come!"

Carol saw Susan's frown of dismay and remembered that they had agreed to deceive — and now she'd come out with the truth to the first person they talked to. She had better modify her statement. Miss Tritt, after all, was one of *them*. "Well, Susan has done a little — three-dimensional work, and I draw a bit. But we're not 'advanced students' by any means."

"Then why did you come here?

There must be dozens of courses for beginners in London."

"Yes, there are, in dingy back rooms. It's our holidays, and when I saw the ad — *park-like surroundings* and so on — we wanted to get out of Town."

"So you pretended to be artists? Good for you." She chuckled again. "Don't you worry. I shan't give you away. If they find out — well, Mr Flavell is a real gentleman. But if you'd rather they didn't know, I'll show you all I've learned in my four years and perhaps you'll get away with it."

"What have you done so far?"

"Well, at first — that's when they took beginners — we had to draw things. Boxes with shadows and pieces of fruit, all before we were allowed to touch colour. Mr Flavell said not all schools do it, but he thinks it essential to start with the basics. And we did a thing called perspective — that's railway lines and roofs, you know. I didn't like it much."

"Here's another arrival," called the

31

woman by the window.

"Oh, really, Myra? That'll be Josephine Satterley. What's she like? Excuse me, girls." Miss Tritt got up and hurried over to look out. "Ooh, Mr Flavell himself is going out to meet her."

Carol and Susan had remained seated. "I'm sorry, Sue," said Carol. "I don't know what came over me. She seemed so harmless and nice that I came out with it before I thought."

"It doesn't matter," said Susan gloomily. "They'll all find out. We were mad to come."

The tall young man with long hair had approached. "Our last member's arrived. Have you met her before, Miss Barton?"

"No," said Carol. "Have you?" What was his name? Mackay, Vance Mackay, that was it. Not a bad-looking chap. That sloppy old pullover was at least clean, and he had an interesting face. He should appeal to Susan.

But he was not looking at Susan, nor she at him. "I don't know her," he said, "but of course I know *of* her. She's the daughter of Martin Satterley, the portraitist. You're familiar with *his* works."

"Am I?" Why couldn't the fellow talk to Susan?

But then the director brought in the new arrival, a young woman with long fair hair, but indistinctive features. She seemed ill at ease when introductions were made.

Carol was more interested in the man accompanying her. So this was John Flavell, the director. She put his age at about forty, for in spite of a youthful figure his hair was greying at the temples. His was an attractive face, with tanned skin, deep-set eyes and clean-cut features. Now he was looking at her and Susan and seemed about to approach, when a gong sounded. Everyone began to move through a sliding door into the adjoining room for dinner. Miss Tritt beckoned Carol and Susan over to one of the three small tables. Mr Flavell sat at another with the newcomer, Josephine Satterley, the elderly man, and Miss Hurst. Mr Mackay and Mr Stein, at the third, were soon joined by a tall angular woman with unnaturally black hair, precisely waved. She had high cheek-bones and must have been beautiful once. Now hard lines pulled down the corners of her mouth, and her forehead was set in a frown. She glanced briefly round the room, with no pretence of friendliness.

"Mrs Flavell," Miss Tritt told them. "She's very clever, you know. She's exhibited all over Europe. Portraits and landscape and still-life. Now *she* might get the Sanderson-Ebbings award, that's *very* likely."

"What's she like?" asked Carol, looking across at the hard profile and set lips. "I mean, as a person?"

"Well — I don't know her very well. She doesn't mix like her husband does.

More reserved, if you know what I mean."

Carol didn't. She had a distinct impression that a cold disdain for inferior talent kept Mrs Flavell from fraternising with Miss Tritt. Yet the woman fascinated her. She had an intellectual face, large dark eyes, and was still undoubtedly handsome. She wore a black dress with an orange neckline, bright orange lipstick, and large round orange dangling earrings. Twin globes, her only jewellery. They swung gently as she moved her head.

"They rotate, you know," said Eva Tritt.

"I beg your pardon?" Carol had a brief vision of whirling orange spheres.

"Mr and Mrs Flavell. They sit at each of the tables in turn."

Carol gathered it was considered an honour to have one of the Flavells at your table — like being on the chosen list of a ship's captain. Miss Tritt was speaking again. "Here's Miss Pillington. Oh, she's coming to *us*."

Miss Pillington was an earnest-looking, middle-aged woman. She wore horn-rimmed glasses and had her mousy-coloured hair pulled back in a workmanlike but unattractive fashion. She greeted them pleasantly but spoke little during the meal. Miss Tritt talked most of the time. The food was served by Mrs Ballins, who waited so deftly on all three tables that there was little delay. "Such a *kind* soul," said Eva Tritt. "She and her husband work very hard and they never complain. I must see if I can help them this time, by doing messages for them in the village."

Coffee was served in the common-room. Eva Tritt stayed with Carol and Susan, like a hen who has found and adopted two stray chicks. There was no hint of unkindness in her tumbling words, and both girls warmed towards her. The tutors were not present. Presumably they took their coffee in the Flavell's quarters. But when the cups had been removed,

Mr Flavell came in and delivered a short speech of welcome. "There will be no lecture or slides tonight, as some of you have come a long way and may be tired after your journey. We start work tomorrow in earnest, and we'll keep you busy then. It's still pleasant outside, if you care to explore the grounds. The boundaries are fenced, but there are two side gates. The one on the northern side leads to our neighbour's estate. The other is up on the plateau at the top of the hill, just this side of the Council quarry. The quarry is idle at present, so you may go through. From above it you can actually see the sea. It's a magnificent view, a favourite with our students. As for our own grounds, feel free to go wherever you please. Many of the old trees are worthy of your study. I should perhaps point out that there is a games-room — the first door down the corridor leading off the entrance hall — with a billiards table, table tennis, darts and so forth. But I warn you, I shall see that you have very little time to use it." He smiled at them and left the room.

"Would you care to go for a stroll?" suggested Eva Tritt. "There's an artificial lake, you know, put in by Mrs Flavell's great-grandfather. It's quite large, and I'm told it's very deep too. Right in the bottom of the valley behind the house."

As they passed through the front hall, she pointed out a lift-shaft in one corner. "It's useful for the Ballins, taking stuff up to the studio. We can go outside through the games-room. This way. There — isn't it beautiful? It used to be the ballroom. What a pity that Mrs Flavell wants to sell up and move."

French doors at one end of the room led out to the side of the house, where a tree-covered slope rose sharply. "That leads to the top of the quarry," explained Miss Tritt. "There's a flat clearing on the summit and we often paint up there. I think it's a pity there aren't any lawns, though, don't you? Just a few sheep to keep the grass down. They could easily afford another gardener, Myra says. I'm sure I don't know. You can't see the lake here at the back until you're through those trees."

She led the way between old oaks and beeches, and they then looked down on the valley at the back of the house, and could see the lake glimmering in the evening light. Grassy slopes, dotted with trees, reached down to it. At the back were grey-green hills. "And there's an old summer-house and a marble statue over there in those trees, and a dove-cot that way and wild flowers of all sorts and a goldfish pond and — come round here — an old orchard, see? There used to be beehives, too, but I didn't see them last year, so I think they've been given away, but it's all so *nice*. There's *such* a lot to paint. Though it's a shame there are no horses or dogs. The stables were all taken down.

But of course, they're *terribly* difficult, horses. Myra says you have to learn all about their bones before you can even *attempt* them."

They walked round to the entrance porch, where Miss Tritt, who was feeling the cold, decided to go in.

Carol sat down on one of the stone animals and looked at Susan. "Well? It's a lovely old house and the grounds are beautiful, and they all seem nice people."

"Not Mrs Flavell," said Susan. "She gives me the creeps. Did you see her at dinner? She looked round at us as if we were so many commodities, multiplying our number by the amount of the fee and deducting income tax and kitchen expenses and calculating what was left."

"No one could possibly look like that. And she may be a very good teacher, so what she thinks doesn't matter. We'll find out tomorrow."

"They'll find *us* out tomorrow."

"Well, they can't send us home, so

don't worry. Are you cold?" Susan had shivered.

"No, not really. It's just — nothing." She could not tell whether the sudden chill she felt was a gust of cold wind or a premonition of danger. "Let's go up to our rooms to unpack and have an early night."

3

THE small notice in each bedroom urging students to be punctual for breakfast had evidently been unnecessary, for such was the enthusiasm of the group that all arrived before eight o'clock in the dining-room. There were no yawns or complaints.

Eva Tritt joined Carol and Susan and chattered as amiably as she had the day before. Had they slept well? Wasn't the bacon good? Those chandeliers were real crystal. Didn't Miss Satterley look pale, poor girl? What did they think of the house?

"It's a fine old building," said Carol, "but the way it's furnished and decorated surprises me. It's as though someone has thrown in a heap of practical furniture without really caring if it matched the house or not. I'd have thought artists would be far more fastidious in their choice."

"It's Mrs Flavell's house," said Eva. "It's been in her family for generations, so I suppose Mr Flavell doesn't like to interfere. She wants to sell it and move out, they say. Wouldn't that be a pity?"

"She may not be interested in interior decorating," said Susan. "Artists seem to specialise, fastening on to one aspect which they like and not bothering about any others. Look at that man Mackay. He's supposed to paint well, but he's so untidy. That awful pullover he wears — and scuffed shoes. Why doesn't he take an artistic pride in his own appearance?"

"Oh dear, like my hair being such a mess," said Eva. "Not that I'm an artist, of course, but I see what you mean. Though Mr Mackay is a poet, isn't he? And that makes *all* the difference. It's a sort of tradition for poets to be untidy. Oh, here's Mr Flavell. The tutors don't take breakfast or lunch with us, so I guess he's come in to talk to everyone."

43

She was right. Mr Flavell explained the position of the studio on the top floor. "Miss Tritt or Miss Hurst can show you the way. Please be there with your materials no later than nine o'clock." He looked ready for work himself. He was wearing a paint-stained jacket and old tweed trousers.

"You see?" said Susan, when he had left the room. "If he was generally artistic, he'd wear something less repulsive."

Carol protested. "Why should he dress to please a bunch of students? I think he looks nice. How old is he? Late thirties? Early forties? His wife looks older, but that may be just her sour expression. Perhaps she's nicer than she looks. Is she, Eva?"

"Well — she seems just a little bossy. She orders her husband about, really quite *rudely* at times. But you can't really judge a person without knowing them well, can you? It wouldn't be fair, and I've never had much to do with her."

Carol interpreted these statements as

a reluctant admission of strong dislike. She looked round the room at the other students. "Mr Sullivan must be the oldest here."

"He's seventy-eight," said Eva. "He told me so last night. What a fine old gentleman! So courteous. That girl Satterley must be the youngest — hardly out of her teens, I'd say. Martin Satterley's daughter, you know. You'd think he'd want to teach her himself, wouldn't you? Mr Stein, now, somewhere in the thirties? It's hard to tell when they wear whiskers."

"He looks German," said Carol. "Hard and ruthless and self-seeking."

"Oh, Germans aren't like that, dear. Why, I've known — "

"Quite different from Mr Mackay," went on Carol. "*He* looks pleasant, intelligent and artistic and kind. And handsome as well," she added for good measure, as she looked for Susan's reaction.

"Potty," pronounced Susan. "Pass the milk please."

So there had been no sudden impact, but that had been too much to hope for. In any case, a slow growing attachment was the sort that lasted best. She would just see that they had plenty of opportunities to be alone together, and leave Nature to do her stuff.

Susan had already dismissed the man Mackay from her thoughts and was looking across at Myra Hurst, who was demolishing a last piece of toast with an air of uncompromising fixity of purpose. Susan watched, fascinated. That poor little piece of bread just didn't stand a chance. Neither would anyone who got in Myra's way. She'd crunch them to bits and spit out the bones.

"Come on, girls," said Eva. "Fetch your stuff and we'll get an early start."

The studio, on the floor above the bedrooms, was a large airy room converted from attics. Skylights and picture windows gave plenty of light, with adjustable blinds and screens to discipline its direction and intensity.

Two lay figures stood in a corner. Easels were stacked in a row. There were sloping desks, flat-topped tables, stools and chairs, and at one end of the room, a dais, presumably for live models. One wall held the lift door and the stairs entrance. From the windows in the other three, in every direction was a magnificent landscape view.

"We forgot to bring smocks," said Carol.

"Use the firm's." Eva pointed to a pile of freshly laundered fawn twill smocks on one of the tables.

Miss Pillington was moving round the room, solemnly helping students with easels and tables, advising on position and checking on materials. She came over to them. "And what are you girls doing?"

Susan suddenly felt like a schoolgirl in her presence. "Abstract," she said nervously, and held out her box of pastels.

Miss Pillington took the box. "Abstract? Unusual choice for abstract, pastels. Should be interesting. Hm — not the best make, but they'll do. A desk, I think, rather than this easel. Here, I'll help you. And a chair. And this stool for your pastels. Now, Miss Barton, is it?"

"I'm trying water-colour for the first time," said Carol boldly, "and as I shall be merely getting the feel of the medium this morning I shan't bother with an easel either." Miss Pillington nodded, and helped her bring forward one of the smaller desks. "Boards and drawing-pins over there. Now your brushes and paints? Ah yes. That's a good rigger. Didn't you bring a chisel? Borrow one from the table stock."

The sun was shining through the large windows now. Miss Pillington looked at it critically, as if it had no right to intrude without permission, then marched over to pull at one of the blinds.

"Why do I need a chisel?" asked Carol. "To scrape off my mistakes?"

"A chisel-shaped brush," explained

Eva. "Like this, see?"

"I'm scared," said Susan. "I feel I'm back at school and haven't done my homework."

"Try to appear confident," Carol exhorted her. "Remember your cane tray they displayed in the school hall. You're an experienced artist but have never before attempted abstract. Bluff it out. You'll get by."

All the students were present by this time, and Mr Flavell mounted the dais to ring a small bell for attention. "Good-morning, ladies and gentlemen. As those of you who have attended previous courses will know, we spend the first day in the studio even when the weather is as delightful as this. You are all experienced and accomplished artists, but in order for us to further your capabilities, we must know the direction of your talent and your present aim. You'll see a still-life arrangement on the stand there if you care to use it. Otherwise I suggest an imaginary landscape. I need not point

49

out why that is of more value than a direct representation in giving us an idea of your particular bent and your preferred technique." He stepped down and began talking to Miss Pillington.

The dreaded moment had come for Susan, but Carol was prepared to enjoy the deceit and her eyes were twinkling merrily. Mr Flavell approached. "Now, you two young ladies? Miss Meadows? And Miss Barton? What is your particular line?" He looked at each and smiled, his deep grey eyes wrinkling at the corners. It was Carol who answered, as Susan sat nervously clutching her box of pastels.

"My friend and I have come for different reasons. Susan here is a black and white artist. She wants to work in pastels and try her hand at some abstract art. I wish to do water-colour. I've never used it before."

Mr Flavell frowned slightly. "Abstract? I favour representational work myself. Miss Pillington will be of more use to you than I, Miss Meadows. So you've specialised in black and white? Pen and ink or pencil?"

Susan's mouth opened a little and stayed there.

"Both," said Carol firmly. "And of course — " Whatever else was black? "Black dye and charcoal and — things."

Mr Flavell's eyebrows rose. "Indeed? You've exhibited, Miss Meadows?"

Susan faltered. "No."

"Once only," intervened Carol. "In St Margaret's hall, in the north."

"And you, Miss Barton? Miss Pillington tells me you have to date confined your work to oils only?"

"I haven't tried anything else," said Carol truthfully.

"But you'll have had initial grounding in other mediums? Where did you originally study? Was water-colour not included in the course?"

"Unfortunately no," Carol told him. "I took a course at a private establishment and the curriculum was limited." It had actually comprised English, History,

51

Geography, Mathematics and French, with one P.T. period a week.

"Well, you'll soon adapt. Water-colour is a delightful medium in the right hands. No doubt, like so many others, you've considered oils more durable. That's not the case, you know. Any pigment — oil, tempera, acrylic — will deteriorate if not properly cared for. If you use reliable colours and protect your work, there's no limit to the permanency."

"I hadn't really considered that aspect."

"You'll find water-colour more difficult, as you no doubt realise. You will, of course, be aware of the main change of approach — light to dark instead of dark to light. Pans, I see?" He took up one of her paints. "I consider tubes preferable, but you'll decide that later for yourself. This was the palette recommended to you? Yes, quite adequate, though I don't favour Payne's Grey for finished work. It tends to fade. And I should have included alizarin. Now I'll leave you to it."

Carol watched him walk away. "He's rather a dear, isn't he? He has awfully nice eyes."

"I'm scared of them all," said Susan. "An imaginary landscape? I don't even know where to begin."

"It's all right for *you*. Draw a few lines and a dot, or a drunken triangle with a fish in it. *I've* got to produce a picture. Well, here goes." She pinned a piece of paper on to her board. "And he thinks I'm aiming at permanency for posterity! Mountains are blue in pictures, I know that much. I'll have lots of blue mountains at the back." She wet her brush, stirred it in the prussian blue pan, and drew a brilliant streak across her paper. "Oh, hell, that's not what I meant. How can I tone that down? Let's try some of this dark brown on top."

Susan timidly took up a red pastel and slowly drew a curved line from NNE to SW. "How's that?"

"Excellent," said Carol. "Really

significant. Give it a blue tributary or put a purple square on it."

The sun was stronger now. Where it had been permitted to enter it made bright geometric patterns on the bare wooden floor. The room was quiet, even Miss Tritt was too absorbed in her work to chatter. The three tutors were moving from one student to another, discussing work in subdued tones. Susan and Carol were mercifully left alone for the first fifteen minutes. Susan thickened her line and put a bulge in the middle. Then it looked a little like a recently fed boa constrictor, so she gave it a bright green eye.

Carol had scrapped her first attempt and started again. Her mountains were paler, but she had added a yellow foreground and an emerald green structure at the right-hand side. The effect was hideous.

Susan looked at it. "That green thing. Is it a tree?"

"Of course it's a tree, you ninny. Anyone can see it's a tree."

"It needs to be pruned. That little trunk couldn't possibly stand the weight of all the funny green stuff on top."

"How are you two getting on?" Eva Tritt left her easel and came over. She looked at Carol's picture. "Oh," she said. Then "Oh," again.

"I know," said Carol. "*Oh*, indeed. What shall I do about it?"

"They'll come any moment," groaned Susan. "And they'll proclaim, 'Stop work, everyone! We have imposters in our midst.'"

"They'll probably let you do a bit more before they come to you, since you've said you're both starting a new medium." Eva looked at Susan's paper. "Oh, lordie! I can't help *you*, Susan. But — " she looked again at Carol's and laughed — "I think we can do a little better than that. Now take another piece of paper. No, that paper's too good to waste, so just turn it over and use the back. Pin it firmly on to your board. Is it stretched?"

"Huh?"

"It's such heavy quality that it may not need it. Look, find your yellow ochre and put a thin layer all over your sheet and leave it to dry. No, thinner — water it down. That's better. I'll be back."

Carol went over to see Eva's own work while her yellow ochre was drying, and found a pleasant landscape already taking shape. Eva was far more competent than she had made herself out to be.

For the next half-hour Carol painted to order. "Cobalt at the top — thin it as you go down, now some pale lemon — no, no, very pale — rinse your brush, dry it and mop out some clouds. See? — not just in the middle like that — there, that's better. I'll show you later what to mix for the shadows on them — now pale blue for the distant hills — paler than that — mauve in front for the nearer ones — mix crimson and cobalt. What would you like in the foreground? Try reeds or something simple, and make the colours stronger."

After Eva had bustled several times from her own work to Carol's, a landscape, actually recognisable as such, had appeared on Carol's paper. Susan had added scales to her boa constrictor, but as it must be abstract, she had not drawn them on his back, but lined them up in a neat row in the upper right hand corner. She made each a different colour and was beginning to enjoy herself.

Miss Pillington was suddenly at her side. She stared long and earnestly at Susan's picture. "Ah," she said finally. Then she stared again. Carol stopped her own painting to watch, hoping that 'Ah' meant something different from 'Oh'. Then, "Yes," said Miss Pillington. "Indeed, yes. You intend to emphasise the fluency rather than aim for a dramatic effect?"

"Oh *yes*," said Susan fervently.

"I think you're right. I shall be most interested to see the finished work. We can discuss it more fully then. In the meantime — " She stared again, then pointed with her pencil to the row of scales. "I should not try to be multi-evocative in this instance. It would destroy the effect of the simple sweep of meaning."

She looked briefly at Carol's landscape but made no comment. Then she passed on.

Eva hurried over. "What did she say?"

"Nothing about my picture," said Carol, "and I think it's so nice. But she liked Susan's."

"I don't think she does much water-colour," said Eva. "Here's Mrs Flavell. She's the water-colour expert. Do you mind if I stay and listen?"

"Please do. It's your painting really."

Mrs Flavell looked disapproving even before she reached them. It was hard to tell whether the sour twist to her lips was a natural feature or the result of some inner distaste for her job. She started accusingly, "You're Miss Barton."

"I know," said Carol childishly. She didn't like the woman.

"Hm — hot pressed, I see?"

"Oh, yes, we're very busy."

Eva broke in hurriedly. "I was just saying to Miss Barton that her hot-pressed paper is really too good for practising in a new medium."

"Paper over there." Mrs Flavell pointed. "Help yourself." She stared at Carol's picture for a few seconds without speaking, then walked off, and a little later was talking vigorously to her husband, whom she had beckoned away from Rudolph Stein.

"She doesn't like me," said Carol.

"I don't like *her*," said Susan. "She didn't say nice things about my snake."

Carol fetched a sheet of paper from the table and began all over again, trying to remember what Eva had told her. The result was far from pleasing. The sky had streaks and patches, the clouds heavy outlines which were not meant to be there.

Both she and Susan were glad when

the little bell was rung again and Mr Flavell announced a break. "We take a rest at this point for coffee, and then I want you to move round and look at one another's efforts. Please don't be shy. You'll be living together for the next three weeks, and the sooner you get well acquainted the better. Don't be afraid to express an opinion of others' work or methods. Or to ask for, or give, advice. You all have something to give, and you all — we all — have something to learn. We share our knowledge here. You may have picked up a trick of technique or learned from experience how to achieve a special chiaroscuric effect. You can help one another more than you realise."

All were downing tools, wiping hands and moving over to the trolley brought up in the lift by Mrs Ballins, who was now pouring tea and coffee. There was a large plate of buttered scones.

The students took their cups with them as they moved to one another's easels, most of them diffidently at first. Myra Hurst was the exception, and her voice could be heard clearly above the rest. "Intriguing illumination there." — "My god, that haze is well done." — "Can't say I like your predominance of shadow in the middle distance."

By keeping near others' work, Susan and Carol avoided discussion of their own. They passed from easel to easel. The standard was frighteningly high. Rudolph Stein had chosen the still-life and already finished a rendering in which the subject matter was recognisable, yet transformed by intensified light and shade into a patterned design. It fascinated Susan. Vance Mackay had painted young birch trees, their feathery leaves and delicate slim branches reflected in a pond. There was something ethereal and fairy-like about them. "It's just beautiful," said Carol in admiration. "Is it the pale colours you've chosen that produce that dreamy effect?"

"Do you like it?" said Vance. "I'm

so awfully glad. I was quite pleased with it myself."

"There's such *feeling* in it."

"Do you really think so? I wanted there to be. There's something so ineffably moving about young birch trees, don't you agree? Like innocent young adolescents, stretching up their arms in hope and trust."

"He's bananas," commented Susan as they moved on. "The adolescents *I* know don't do that with their arms."

"He's a poet, and that's the way the world appears to him. And his painting is one of the most beautiful I've ever seen."

Myra Hurst's painting was as yet indeterminate, with strong patches of colour and firm lines, which seemed to express her own personality — decisive, aggressive, emphatic. Mr Sullivan's was in traditional style, with muted, harmonious colours, detailed and precise in the finished portions. Miss Satterley had chosen the still-life, but her interpretation was more realistic and less interesting than that of Stein. Each picture was impressive in its own way, and Carol realised how hopeless was the task of trying to learn a lifetime's work in three weeks. She said to Josephine Satterley, "That looks awfully good to me. Are you enjoying it here?"

"No," said the girl coldly.

"What's the matter? I'd love to be able to paint like that."

"I don't like painting," said Josephine. "I loathe painting." She glared at Carol as if holding her personally responsible for the fact.

"Then why did you come?"

"Because my father insisted. If Daddy paints, daughter must paint. That's his simple logic."

"But you're good."

"I ought to be. He's worked on me long enough. But he doesn't do water-colour and he sent me for that, and for what he calls the 'fresh approach' of other tutors. He wants to take me with him next year on a painting tour in the south of France."

"That sounds marvellous. I can't see your objection."

"Can't you?" Josephine shrugged and turned away.

"Back to work, please," called Mr Flavell. Then he walked over to Carol's and Susan's corner and was gazing at their work when they arrived. He looked up at each of them in turn, his mouth twitching slightly at the corners. It was very much as though he were trying not to laugh. Then he looked back at the paintings and stroked his chin. Carol decided to save him the effort of composing a tactful remark. She said, "I think I should like to start right from the beginning, just as though I'd never done any painting before."

He looked relieved. "A very wise decision, Miss Barton. If you care to do the same, Miss Meadows, as a change from your pastels, there are spare brushes and tubes of water-colour on the shelves there. Students' grade but quite good enough for initial practice. Start with washes and then do a colour chart. And try out every type of brush. You can't express yourself adequately in any medium without first learning to handle your tools." He passed on to Mr Stein.

"Washes?" said Susan. "I guess he's right. I didn't know I'd get myself so grubby." She had a smudge of green on her cheek, more than one colour in her fair hair, and her borrowed smock, where she had wiped her hands, was a garish display of all the hues in her box.

"Good lord, you *are* in a mess. But I don't think he was ordering you to the bathroom. Let's ask Eva."

Eva laughed. "I heard. You two are under suspicion. You're to practise washes of colour. Trying to get even tone, then a gradated one, then colours merging."

"And the colour chart?"

"I'll show you. You'll enjoy it and it'll keep you busy for the rest of the day. Take one of those large sheets and rule it into squares — "

By the time lunch was announced, both girls were completely absorbed in their work. Washes covered numerous sheets of paper. Mr Flavell had visited them only once again, when he merely recommended a larger brush to hold more colour and advised on the tilt of the paper.

"He knows," said Susan. "He was laughing at us."

"Well, he didn't order us out. This is fun, isn't it?"

They sat with Eva and Rudolph at lunch, and the conversation turned inevitably to painting.

"You're doing abstract, Miss Meadows?" Stein's voice was deep, his words clipped and precise, and he had an earnestness of manner which suggested intense interest in whatever subject occupied him at the time. "Pastels was an unusual choice for abstract, was it not?"

"I suppose so," said Susan. "But I'm doing watercolour washes for the rest of the day. I'll get back to pastels tomorrow."

"I see." He took the butter with an air of deep concern, as if pondering its shape and origin.

"Are you a professional artist, Mr Stein?"

"No. Art is only my hobby. Sculpture mostly."

"And such a successful hobby," said Eva. "You won the Porter prize twice, didn't you? Once for your famous *Woman with Spoon*. He's awfully good, girls."

Stein did not comment. He was cutting himself a symmetrically even piece of cheese.

The afternoon passed quickly. There was no coffee-break, but work stopped at 4.30. They assembled in the common-room later, to await dinner at seven. Most had changed for dinner tonight, all were more relaxed. An excellent sherry was served before the meal and the food was good. Carol and Susan sat with Eva and were again joined by Miss Pillington. Did the tutors choose their table, Carol wondered, or draw lots? Miss Pillington looked as reserved as usual, but Eva's happy chatter soon had her talking about her experiences in Italy, where she had met, and worked with, a number of well-known artists. She spoke without conceit, giving a factual account of her own career. Carol liked her, but guessed at some disappointment or tragedy in her life which had resulted in her sedate attitude. She had clear blue eyes behind the glasses, and her features were regular. She could even be pretty if she softened by another hair style the hard aspect her face presented.

Mr Flavell spoke at the end of the meal. There would be no criticism session tonight, as many were still getting the feel of their new medium. Carol could have sworn he cast an amused glance at her as he said this. There would be a short talk by his wife on a couple of modern artists, but attendance was not obligatory.

All, however, were present at the lecture. Mrs Flavell spoke well, succinctly giving facts, and her husband showed slides when she signalled. It was a well-prepared talk and should have been of interest, but Susan and Carol were not the only ones stifling yawns, not from boredom, but from physical fatigue.

"I had no idea painting was so exhausting," said Susan as they walked up to their rooms later.

"It's good, though, isn't it? And they didn't throw us out."

"Yes, it's nice. But there's something — just something — "

"You didn't like the coffee? Your bed is lumpy?"

"The bed is very comfy and I drank tea. No, it's just a feeling I had when I arrived."

"You were scared stiff they wouldn't let us stay."

"Not that. Something else. A sort of vague impression which was frightening and it's still with me."

"It'll be gone by morning. Eva says we go outside on the second day."

"That will be pleasant," said Susan doubtfully. "Good-night." Her shoulders were drooping a little as she turned into her room.

4

MR FLAVELL mounted the dais. "Good-morning, ladies and gentlemen. Those of you who have attended the course before know that the second day is devoted to a comparison of methods. We all portray the same scene so that we can benefit by a subsequent examination of interpretation and technique. On such a lovely day as this we'll work outdoors. The lake is the chosen subject for your efforts, but the angle and height from which you view it is your own choice, a choice which itself will be a reflection of your individuality, so set up where you please. Easels, desks and chairs have been taken down there. Aim to have a completed sketch by half-past three, when we return to the studio for comparison and criticism, considering in turn the intention and impact of each painting, as well as the technique employed. There will be no advice given during the day unless you ask for it, because it's important for the purpose of the exercise that you give free expression to your response to the subject-matter."

He stepped down from the dais and came straight over to Carol. "Don't waste your d'Arches, Miss Barton. Help yourself to the paper over there." He turned to Susan. "Your abstract interpretation of our lake should be most interesting, Miss Meadows." He grinned openly and left them.

"We were mad to think we could get away with it," said Susan.

"What does it matter? We're here to learn, and that's what we'll do. Eva's taught me a lot already. Come on, it'll be lovely outside."

The man-made lake in the valley below the house fitted so naturally into the landscape, seemed so essentially a part of it, that it could have been formed thousands of years ago, when the hills themselves took shape. As Carol and Susan strolled down the grassy slope towards it, they were joined by Myra Hurst, whose long stride easily overtook them.

"Decent sort of day, what? You haven't been before. Enjoying it?"

"Yes, thank you," said Susan.

"You're the abstract, eh? Saw your work yesterday. The Pillington likes it. Can't be bothered with abstract myself."

Susan tried to remember some of Ralph Hopkins' phrases. "It's a matter of understanding it, isn't it? Appreciating the message of the artist?"

Myra snorted. "Fooling the public, that's what it is. One mighty fake. Don't mean you," she added to Susan. "*You* can't help it if you like that junk. Not your fault." She spoke with the pity a healthy person would show to an unfortunate with a club-foot or cast eye.

"There must be something in it," protested Susan. "Mr Stein says modern art has either meaning or design, and some of it is meant to arouse emotion rather than express it."

"Huh! Man's a fool. Told me yesterday that Cox should have stuck to water-colour instead of listening to Muller." She glanced at Susan and mistook her puzzled expression for amazed shock. "Aha, that knocks you, eh? He did, though. He said just that. Has some weird ideas, that fellow."

Carol thought it wise to change the subject. "Have you been here before, Myra?" She wondered if she should have said 'Miss Hurst'. In any other gathering they would all have been using first names by now, but there was something formal and old-world about the atmosphere here. Perhaps it was the influence of the lovely old home.

"Three times," said Myra. "Doesn't teach me much, but the concentrated painting for three weeks does me good. Can't sneak off to golf or horse-riding. Stuck here and have to paint. Good discipline."

She did not look as if she needed any help with self-discipline. Her strong chin and decisive manner gave the impression of an iron will, capable of forcing herself and others to its command.

"But the tuition is good, isn't it?" asked Carol.

"Very good, for those who need it. Mrs Flavell's had a lot of success. Exhibited on the Continent. Won the Merles prize. Can't stand the woman. Like to throttle her at times. But she has talent. Can't deny that."

"She doesn't seem to enjoy teaching."

"No. Don't know why she does it. Vanity, I guess. Stacks of money. Doesn't need the fees. Heard she wants to sell up. Pity. Family home."

"And her husband? Is he a good artist too?"

"Not up to her standard, but pretty good. Hot on seascapes. Gets more commissions than she does. Don't know why. Work appeals more, for some reason. Pillington knows her stuff too. Good teacher, sound. All aspects — even that crazy abstract. They're all three in the running for the Sanderson-Ebbings award."

"Yes, we've heard that. What — " Carol stopped. No doubt it was a well-known award which she, as an artist, should know of. Instead she asked, "Are you also?"

Myra frowned. "Don't know if I qualify. Born in Winchester. Giving it a go, mind you. Both the Flavells have got a good show. You know, I wouldn't be surprised if the Pillington took the job here to see what the competition was like. In the enemy's camp, you might say." She laughed, a loud horsy neigh.

"Well, of course the award is worth striving for, isn't it?" asked Carol as a leading question.

"I'll say. Tour of four countries, all expenses paid and a few hundred quid spending money. Wouldn't mind it myself. Well, see you."

They were at the lake-side now, and

Myra strode off to fetch an easel. Yes, she certainly *would* like that award. Blast being born in the wrong county. But they didn't ask for birth certificates, surely? She'd lived in Sussex nearly all her life. She had as good a chance as anyone else in other respects. There were only three or four entrants who were not here on the course, and from what she had heard they wouldn't be in the running. As for the ones here — she was glad she'd persuaded John Flavell to get them all to the same session. Just as well to know what you're up against. Old Sullivan — poor old dotard didn't have a show. Stein — known for his sculpture, not his painting. It was a painting award, so one could write him off, if he'd bothered to enter. Young Satterley was the real danger, being so young, and with her father's influence. Well, nothing came easily. You had to fight for it. She hadn't got where she was by shrinking before difficulties.

The water of the lake was a soft blue under an almost cloudless sky.

Fringed by reeds, shrubs and trees, with a back-drop of hills, it presented a picture which made Carol all the more eager to learn how to reproduce it on paper. There were single features, too, which would have made good pictures in themselves if one only knew how to paint them — a dinghy moored on the lake, a fallen tree, a rotting log, a large rock with smaller ones near it and thick foliage behind.

Eva Tritt was beckoning. "There's a good spot here, girls." So they carried a couple of desks over to her, under the shade of an enormous oak. Miss Tritt fussed round altering the position of their desks. "Keep your work in the shade — that's not level — a fraction to the left."

Then she began to hum happily as she set up her own easel. What a pleasant couple of young women. Good company, polite, and not pushing or loud like so many young folk now. Grateful for a little help, and ready to listen. She would teach them everything she knew, just as the others had taught her. Such *nice* people! What a really lovely day it was! She would do a very pretty scene of the lake, to give her niece, Barbara. She'd have several nice paintings to take home this time. She was making progress, she really was. Myra said so, and she would know. Even Mr Flavell said so, and he never flattered. You always knew where you were with him. Of course, she had that little job to carry out, but it should not be too difficult, she'd find a way and it shouldn't interfere with her painting — well, she couldn't do it in class hours anyway, so she would relax and enjoy herself. Now if she made that cluster of rocks the focal point instead of the lake itself, would that be a good original idea?

The air was still and clear, the sun sparkled on the lake, and Carol had a feeling of content which even the occasional low moan of distress from Susan could not dispel. Best of all, she was left alone, for the three tutors were themselves painting, presumably to demonstrate their individual styles to the class later and to show in how many different ways the same subject could be interpreted.

Morning coffee was brought out by the Ballins, and they all gathered round a table set in the grove of elms. Carol saw Vance Mackay, remembered her proposed use for the man, and manoeuvred Susan over to him.

"I hear you're a well-known poet, Mr Mackay," she began.

"Not really. I'm a journalist, and just a would-be poet, with painting as a hobby. And call me Vance, please. Have you managed to — ?"

"Oh, there's Mr Stein," broke in Carol. "Excuse me. I want to ask him about — " She could not on the spur of the moment think what any woman in her right mind would want to ask the stocky bearded Stein about, so she left the sentence unfinished and walked away. She'd done her part in putting them together. Having said she wanted to speak to Stein, she had to go to where he was talking with Mr Sullivan. The old man nodded politely to her, then took his cup back to the table. He looked pathetically thin and frail, as if the next puff of wind could blow him away.

Rudolph Stein gestured towards him. "He iss a ferry good artist."

"Will he get the Sanderson-Ebbings award?" asked Carol, showing off her knowledge.

"Perhaps, if he is eligible. Are you enjoying the course so far?" His face was earnest, his gaze disconcertingly direct.

"Yes, thank you. Are you an artist by profession, Mr Stein?"

"No." A guarded look came over his face.

"I heard you were a sculptor?"

"Only as a side-line. Are you interested in sculpture?"

"Er — yes."

"Then tell me, do you consider that the Merrythorpe marble in the hall was influenced by the later works of Grossheim?"

"No," said Carol emphatically. She spoke the truth. Such an idea had not entered her head.

"It is an interesting point. If you consider the modelling of the lower limbs and compare it with *Vandal Arrested* — "

"Well, of course, if you do *that*," conceded Carol, wondering how she could escape.

"Grossheim's style itself changed so considerably in his later years. It's amazing how quickly he tired of realistic representation and sought to express his own emotion rather than the visual image before him."

Carol let her mind wander as he spoke. She glanced over at Susan and Vance Mackay, trying to detect some sign of mutual interest. Then the bell sounded and they were ordered back to work.

The rest of the day passed pleasantly. They returned to the house for lunch, but none stayed long, as they were working against time, even those who had apparently finished their picture seeking to make improvements of detail. At 3.30 they packed up.

"What a mess you're in, Sue! You have pastel all over you."

"I know. There's no time to wash either, because we have to go straight to the studio. Thank goodness for these smocks." Susan wiped her hands down the already multi-coloured garment. "Why did you leave me with that moony Mackay? He said my lake looks like a poached egg turned blue with cold."

"Well — as a matter of fact, it does, rather."

"I bet Miss Pillington doesn't think so. And he said your hair has live things in it."

"He WHAT?"

"Don't get shirty. He said it was alive with sunbeams, or some such nonsense. Like I said, moony. He's a poet. I know what your hair's like.

It's very nice hair, but I didn't want to go on and on talking about it."

"I don't blame you. Look, we're packing up just in time. It's going to rain." Clouds were beginning to form over the hills, and there was suddenly a cold chill in the air.

Most of the students carried their own easels or collapsible tables back to the studio, an act of consideration for the Ballins which pleased Carol. Vance Mackay carried hers as well as his own, which did not please her. She had to admit that transporting two tables, his sticky oil painting and a box of materials, was a difficult operation which he handled with admirable ease. But couldn't the silly clot see that Susan was shorter and slighter than she, and more in need of help?

In the studio, each painting was handed to Miss Pillington, who laid it carefully on the floor of the dais. When the Flavells arrived and all were seated, she held up the pictures one by one. Carol was waiting with interest to hear the comments on her own, but Susan's heart was pounding like that of a nervous schoolgirl whose composition on How I Spent My Holidays was about to be read out to the class.

Mr Sullivan's was the first. "A fine piece of work," said Mr Flavell, "by a highly accomplished artist. Note the treatment of the foliage, a field in which Mr Sullivan's expertise is well known. The dexterity of his brushwork is only a small part of his skill. You will admire the sense of vitality in the trees and shrubs. I'm sure you'll all have many specific questions to put to Mr Sullivan this evening."

Miss Pillington and Mrs Flavell endorsed his remarks, and added a few of their own. Then the work of the three tutors was held up, that of each being discussed and evaluated by the other two. The difference in style was obvious to Carol, yet each seemed to her a masterpiece, of a standard which she could never hope to attain.

Myra Hurst's painting was pronounced

'strong and invigorating', that of Mackay praised chiefly for the play of light on the water.

Miss Tritt's was the next to be shown, and even to Carol's untutored eye it was not in the same class. Mr Flavell was honest but kind in his comments. He criticised the composition, praised her progress, and pointed out the 'happy arrangement' of the rocks in the foreground.

When Miss Pillington handed him another, he glanced at Carol with a slight grin. "Miss Barton is a complete beginner in the water-colour medium," he said. "The faults are those to be expected, too obvious to discuss. You can work further on this, Miss Barton. Push back the hills to begin with." He put it down without showing it to the class. "We'll all be interested to see your progress." Several of the others turned to her and smiled encouragingly.

Miss Satterley's work was pale and harmonious. "A subtle impression of melancholy," commented Mr Flavell. "A dreamy pensive atmosphere has been created by a self-imposed limitation of her palette. I'm sure you'll be asked tonight, Miss Satterley, to specify the exact colours used." He compared her work with the 'robust language' of Mr Stein. Stein's scene was recognisable, but as in his still-life of the day before, the shadows and contours had been emphasised in such a way that a pattern had emerged and dominated the picture.

Susan's was the last to be held up. "I can't judge this one," said Mr Flavell. "As you know, I'm not an advocate of what is to me erroneously called 'modern art'. Miss Pillington?"

"A most interesting interpretation," said Miss Pillington. "Miss Meadows is obviously trying to express the intransigent force of nature. She fails, however, in my opinion, to emphasise the inevitable mortality of the foliage. What do you think, Mr Stein?"

"I admire the overall effect," said Stein, "but I can't entirely agree as to the intention of the artist. It'll be interesting tonight to hear Miss Meadows' own exposition of the essential symbolism."

"Indeed, yes," said Mr Flavell. "The paintings can be left here for viewing in the meantime. Unless, Miss Barton, you may wish to work on yours? Water-colour doesn't require the same preparation of materials and you may find time — "

"Don't destroy it," he said to her quietly when she gratefully went up to collect it. "You'll find it of interest in a year's time, if only to emphasise to you the progress you'll have made by then."

Both Susan and Carol felt utterly confused by the time they left the studio. The other students gathered round the paintings for further discussion, except for Eva, who was going to drive to Hastings to pay accounts for the Ballins and buy some groceries for them. "The saving in the supermarket there is really worth the trip, and I'll enjoy the drive."

Carol admired her kindness. She had herself not given much thought to the Ballins, who were, after all, paid servants well rewarded for their work.

Eva was not back in time for dinner, so Carol and Susan sat down at a table with Mr Sullivan, and the fourth chair was soon taken by Mrs Flavell. It was a quiet meal. Mr Sullivan ate slowly, and the process required his full attention. Mrs Flavell was not disposed to talk. Any attempt by Carol to start a conversation was met by a cool polite answer which did not encourage her to continue. She was glad when the meal was over and they went into the common-room for coffee. Rudolph Stein served her and Susan.

"You're not really going to ask me for an explanation of my lake tonight, are you?" asked Susan.

He grinned at her. "I wouldn't dream of it. I don't think either of you need fear questions."

He was right. The evening session was lively and prolonged, but Carol and Susan were not involved. They were impressed by the willingness with which the others answered questions and shared with one another their formulas for admired features of their work, explaining readily which colours had been blended and how a special effect had been achieved.

"They *are* nice people, aren't they?" said Susan later when she and Carol were making tea in her room. "Not mean or envious or conceited."

"I wouldn't include Mrs Flavell in that," said Carol.

"No, perhaps not. And Myra Hurst frightens me a bit. I wouldn't like to get on the wrong side of her. But all the others have been nice to us, and they're decent to one another too. Miss Satterley's stand-offish, but she was answering questions tonight, not keeping any secrets back."

"You wouldn't know if she was. It's that fellow Stein I mistrust. How's your premonition?"

"It isn't exactly a premonition. Just

a sort of feeling. And I *like* Rudolph Stein."

"I wouldn't trust him an inch. Are you sure your 'sort of feeling' isn't just nervousness?"

"Perhaps it is. Anyway, it'll pass."

But when Carol had left Susan sat on the edge of the bed for a while, staring out of the window at the dark outline of the distant hills, thinking over what Carol had said and trying to analyse her strange apprehension. It was surely just some small thing. One day it would crystallise. In the meantime, she must simply ignore it. She would go to bed and put her mind firmly on planning a picture to start in the morning. Perhaps if this time she thought of the title first, and then a design to fit it? *The Scented Splash*? *Hindsight at Dusk*? *Prophet Awakened*? . . .

5

THAT night it rained. It rained heavily, persistently and loudly, as if to make up for time lost. It had stopped by dawn next morning, but the sky was still overcast, and the air chilly.

It was Mrs Flavell who mounted the dais when classes began. "My husband appears to have had a slight accident," she announced, "and will be delayed." With no further explanation she walked down the steps and over to the nearest student, who happened to be Josephine. Such was her air of authority and unapproachable disdain that no one asked for more details.

"An accident!" Carol's voice showed alarm. "I wonder what's happened?"

Susan smiled. "A *slight* accident. Don't look so worried. I believe you've fallen for that fellow."

"Don't talk rot." Carol was annoyed to find herself reddening as she answered, and went on quickly, "But *she* doesn't seem to care. What does she mean, '*appears* to have had an accident'? He either has or he hasn't. It's a silly way to put it. She's a horrible woman."

"Yes, she probably threw the toaster at him, or took a swipe with the bread-knife."

But when Mr Flavell came in half an hour later, it was only his left arm which was in a sling. He had a graze on the side of his face and a streak of mud down the back of his jacket.

"What happened?" asked Carol anxiously, when he came over to their corner. "Is it broken?"

"I don't think so. Just a bad sprain. It's not serious."

"How did you do it?"

He frowned, and was silent a moment before he replied, "I fell. Down part of the quarry."

"How? Did you trip?"

"The clay bank at the top gave way. It must have been undermined by the heavy rain last night. Be careful if you go up there. Anyone could slip. I was fortunate. I landed on a ledge and Ballins was within call. He helped me up. But enough of that. What would you like to do today? I suggest you try some simple sketches for harmony of colour and composition. They are the essentials of good painting, and if you can master them you'll be well on the way. The mechanics of applying paint will develop later. I'm not going to give you any advice on composition at this stage. I'd prefer to see what your own taste will produce. Do several sketches, and keep them simple. Then we'll discuss them."

When he had moved on, Susan looked up. "How could he fall? He shouldn't be drunk at this hour of the morning."

"Anyone could have fallen. He said so. The ground's undermined. What a good thing it's his left arm. At least he can still paint. I wonder if it is broken? He didn't seem sure."

"He may be left-handed," said Susan wickedly, and watched the look of alarm on her friend's face, then the relieved expression when she evidently remembered he was not. "What was he doing up there, anyway?"

"Painting, I suppose. All his day's taken up with tutoring us, and he has to do his own stuff in the early morning or after classes."

"You'd think he would have painted every possible view for miles around here by now."

"Yes, but he and his wife have commissions, Eva says. They're well known, and it's fashionable to order a painting from one of the Flavells."

"If he paints up there so often he should know better than to teeter on the edge. That was idiotic."

"You have to go fairly close to the edge to get a good view of the sea, they say. And the ground gave way. He wasn't teetering and he's *not* an idiot. As he said, it could've happened to anyone."

Susan relented. "All right. I didn't really mean it. Look at that streak of mud on the back of his coat. He didn't even bother to change — just wrapped his arm up and came in to teach. That was probably to annoy his wife. Eva says she was sneering at his 'filthy outfit' the other day and asking why he didn't wear a smock like everyone else."

"Poor chap. Men have their favourite jackets. And it's only paint-stained, not dirty. At least, it was until now, and that mud will brush off when it dries. Why *should* he change if he doesn't want to? He didn't look at your work, did he?"

"No. He doesn't approve of abstract. Neither do I really. Whose silly idea was it that I do abstract? But I think I'm learning something about colour and design."

"You're doing fine," said Carol loyally. "Those — er — geese? and the — bicycle handlebars? — anyway, I'm sure it's good."

When John Flavell returned she asked again about his arm, but he refused to discuss it. He looked with interest at the three quick sketches she had done. "Yes, that's the idea. The combination of colours in this one is quite pleasing, and there are no glaring faults of composition in any of them. You obviously have a sense of balance. In fact, the arrangement *here* is too good. The items look set up, artificial. Your role must always be *make it look natural*. Now how can you improve this? How can you make it look natural?"

"A rock there?" Carol pointed. "Or a tree-stump? Or a girl in a flowing gown lying down reading a novel?"

He laughed. "You may find the last a little difficult as yet. But you have the right idea." He looked over at Susan's bright display colour and grinned. "I'm afraid I can't tell you how to make *that* look natural, Miss

97

Meadows. I'm leaving your tuition to Miss Pillington."

Carol worked with enthusiasm all day, and to her amazement as well as pleasure John Flavell finally said, in a tone of surprise, "Do you know, Miss Barton, I think you show promise."

"Honest? *Me?*"

"I don't flatter." He was turning over her pile of sketches done during the day, staring earnestly at some, nodding at others. "I can't be sure yet, but you show certain indications. We'll get you on to basics tomorrow — brushwork, paper preparation, colour mixing, textures, some of the simpler tricks of the trade — and then see how you go."

"That'll be great. Have you forgiven us for coming under false pretences?"

His eyes twinkled. "You had the cheek of the devil. But I admire your gumption. And who knows? You may be an artist before you leave."

Carol very much doubted it as she listened to the experienced students chatting after class. Not only were many of the terms they used foreign to her, the opinions they expressed and the observations they made were sometimes incomprehensible. The talk that evening was given by Miss Pillington. It was about a famous artist called Marcel Duchamp, who drew a moustache and beard on a reproduction of the Mona Lisa, which action was immediately hailed as an achievement of penetrating criticism, proving conclusively the homo-sexuality of Leonard da Vinci. She didn't understand. The reaction of her teachers at grammar school had been quite different when she had disfigured Cromwell in her History text-book. Yes, there were some facets of art which would always be beyond her.

In spite of this, the next few days were very happy, the happiest of the course. The weather became fine again, and they painted outside much of the time. Carol could see herself improving as she applied the techniques she was learning, and her obvious progress was a spur to further effort. Susan, too, was becoming absorbed in her work, and was now glad that she had chosen abstract art. Mrs Flavell ignored her. Mr Flavell, when he looked at her pictures at all, was inclined to laugh, but he admitted prejudice and urged her to persevere. Rudolph Stein helped with both encouragement and suggestions, and she found to her astonishment that whatever she drew seemed to win some praise from Miss Pillington. She was learning to blend her pastels and to choose her combinations of colour with care. Even Carol admired her green and brown design with the circles and truncated pyramids. "It's quite pleasant to look at," she admitted. "I'd certainly rather have that on my wall than *Emotion 25*."

"Would you really? Miss Pillington says it displays heretic sentiment in the interweaving of the circles."

"It does? How nice. What does she mean?"

"I've no idea. It looks to me like

a dish-mop. Rudolph was enthusiastic. He said something about exuberant sensuality."

"That sounds rather coarse in a dish-mop. But I like the colours."

"Your own work is smashing now, Carol."

"Far from it. But I'm learning. Painting makes one more observant. Do you know, Sue, I looked out the window this morning, and instead of thinking how pretty it all is, I found myself saying cobalt in those elm trunks, Prussian blue with a dash of raw sienna for the gum, Winsor green rather than Hooker's for the grass in this early light."

It must have been obvious to all that Carol was no artist, but none commented on the fact, and when she asked for advice it was readily given. Eva Tritt was particularly helpful, because she was near the beginner's stage herself and did not overlook elementary difficulties which the others might not have thought worthy of mention. Mrs Flavell was quick to point out mistakes and demonstrate their correction. With no sign of genuine interest, almost with an imperious indifference, she would take Carol's brush from her and in a few scornful strokes could convert an apparently hopeless mess into an attractive picture. She commented on brush strokes and colours, and suggested exercises which Carol carried out, but somehow made Carol feel that her efforts were a waste of everyone's time, as she would never achieve anything worth while.

John Flavell, on the other hand, seemed genuinely pleased with her progress. He spent a lot of time with her, and she found herself making special efforts to produce something which would win praise from him. He constantly stressed the need for good balance and focus of attention. "See those four trees in a straight line under that cloud? It's natural, it's there, but if you painted them like that it would not *look* natural." Carols liking and respect for him grew, as did her sympathy, for even in the presence of the students Mrs Flavell spoke to him in a tone which was scathing and hostile. His arm was still in a sling, and Carol argued with him. "If it *is* broken and sets itself wrongly you may have trouble with it all your life."

"I have no time to waste on finding out," he told her. "It's not my painting hand, and it'll mend in time. It's a darned nuisance, certainly, because I can't even hold a tooth-brush in it yet, but I'm coping. I've become quite expert at dressing one-handed. Now don't you see that the shadow you've put under that rock detracts from the effect of the dark oak branches? — "

Myra Hurst was helpful in another way. Myra was a fighter, one who would never give up, and she could pass on her determination. "Of course you have difficulties. Don't we all? Hell, girl, you've got to battle a problem, not run from it. There's always *something* you can do. Like riding cross-country.

If your damned nag won't jump a stream, you ride him through it or look for a bridge. If he balks at a fence, you find a way round it, or knock the fence down. All right, so you can't wash out that ugly furze bush you were stupid enough to put in. You're stuck with it. So what? Emphasise it, enlarge it, make it your focal point, or else scrap the whole bloody picture and start again. But *don't give up*."

There was a general atmosphere of friendly cooperation, and as the group's initial reserve relaxed comments were outspoken and frank. Most confessed not to understand Susan's efforts, and made fun of them, but not unkindly. Myra's opinion was often sought, for her remarks were particularly forthright, unequivocal, and unhampered by any desire to please. One could not always agree with Myra's views, but they were helpful through their uncompromising sincerity. She and Stein argued constantly and vehemently, but without any noticeable animosity.

Eva remained cheerful, voluble and kind. She had again driven into Hastings to fix up accounts and other business for the Ballins, and even Mrs Flavell thawed a little under her obvious readiness to give help wherever she could. There was no doubt that Eva was enjoying the course.

Mr Sullivan was happy too. He wore a contented half-smile as he painted. His quiet courteous manner, and his diffidence about his work, would not lead one to suspect that he was an artist of such renown. It was known, that he, Miss Pillington, the Flavells, Myra and Josephine were all on the short list for the Sanderson-Ebbings award.

"What *is* it?" Carol asked Eva one day. "And why are so many of the candidates gathered here?"

"It's a big art grant, open only to residents of Sussex, born in Sussex. Old Colonel Sanderson-Ebbings was a millionaire who lived near Horsham. He died last year and this grant is one of several bequests to the arts. Isn't it exciting? There's only ten in the running for it. They published a list in the paper. And *six* of them are here with us!"

"That's what I don't understand. Why are they? They could be suspected of trying to copy tricks of technique — you know, like industrial espionage. And the Flavells wouldn't want to spoil their own chances by giving them tips."

"Oh, John Flavell's not like that at all. He and Mr Sullivan have been exchanging advice. I've heard them. Besides, it's awarded only partly on past accomplishments, from what I've heard. There's a three-hour practical as well, and a panel of judges will choose the best. Attendance at this school could be an additional qualification, because it's the best in the county, and it's known right throughout England. Aren't we *lucky* to be here? Among all these *famous* artists?"

"Isn't it an odd coincidence that four

entrants are here at the same time?"

"Oh, that's not a coincidence at all. Myra says that once they applied John Flavell wrote to them suggesting they all come to the same session so they could meet one another. Wasn't that a *nice* thing to do?"

"So we're in distinguished company!" said Carol. "Two complete beginners! No wonder John Flavell was amused. But there must be some jealousy and ill-feeling among the competitors."

"I haven't noticed it," said Eva. "Such *nice* people all of them. So kind and helpful. Of course, Mrs Flavell — but then she's a wonderful painter."

Dear old Eva, thought Carol. She can't even speak unkindly of that detestable woman.

Mrs Flavell was very difficult to like. But she was a wonderful painter, as Eva said. Carol would stand for minutes before one of her framed pictures, trying to analyse its charm. And the woman was decorative herself. She wore a tailored smock during classes and was one of those very few artists who are able to retain clean hands. She dressed for dinner every evening, and her clothes exuded elegance. She was coldly polite to the students, showing clearly that socially they did not come up to her minimum standard requirements. They were not the *right* people, explained Vance, the polished people, those who were fashion-conscious, who knew a Rye Lane from a Torino, and who could talk easily and at length on any subject of which they knew nothing. Carol had not heard him speak so bitterly before, and wondered if a personal clash with Mrs Flavell had roused his anger.

She was disappointed in Vance for another reason. He showed less interest in Susan than in her, and was failing to fulfil the role she had chosen for him. She wanted to shout at him sometimes when he brought her coffee or set up her table, "Not *me*, you twit! *Her*." Moreover, Susan appeared indifferent to him, which was a pity, as he was handsome enough, with his thick dark hair and lively eager eyes.

But if Susan were heart-broken over being jilted, she was hiding it well. She had a new animation and gaiety which was good to see. "I'm developing obtundescence," she told Carol happily one day. "Miss Pillington says so. What is it?"

"Swelling, I think. You shouldn't have cream on your dessert."

"No, it's something to do with backgrounds, and it's very clever, but I don't know what it is. I must ask Rudy."

Rudolph Stein was seeking Susan's company too often for Carol's liking. "Ask *him*? What for? He's a German. He has a hard teutonic face. Notice his cold blue eyes? You keep away from that fellow."

"He has a firm masterful appearance, and I like his eyes."

"He doesn't say anything about his past. I bet he was a double agent during the war."

"How could he be? He wasn't born then. He's only thirty-four."

"How do you know?"

"He told me. He tells me lots of things."

"He's a crook on the run. That's why he wears a beard."

"Every second man has a beard these days," said Susan indignantly. "I like his beard. And he's not a German. He was born in Salisbury."

"Then why has he an accent?"

"I haven't noticed it."

"I'm not surprised. It comes and goes. He's a phoney, Susan. Either he's a German pretending not to be, or he's not and he wants us to think he is. Either way it's fishy and you shouldn't have anything to do with him."

"He's very nice to talk to, and we have a lot in common."

"What could you possibly have in common with *him*?"

"We both like fried mushrooms."

"That's hardly the basis for a lasting friendship. You're always buzzing off going for walks with the fellow lately."

"Why not? He wants me to go down the valley after class this afternoon to show me how to make abstracts from landscape. I said I would."

"Well, you be careful. Don't let him pump you about the plans for that nuclear reactor they're building near Birmingham."

Susan smiled. "I shan't, I promise. What are you going to do?"

"Play table tennis with Vance, I suppose. He's always asking me to."

"He's hooked on you, isn't he?"

"Of course not. Don't be silly."

"Well, he's written a poem about you. About those things in your hair."

"I wish you wouldn't talk of my hair like that. How do you know he has, anyway?"

"He dropped a piece of paper and I picked it up. It's about you, I'm sure it is. Like to hear it?"

"No, I would not."

"Listen." Susan pulled a piece of paper from the pocket of her smock.

"It's torn off. There's something *languid heart*. Then it goes on

> Her very presence can eclipse
> The mocking moon of care.
> There is laughter on her lovely lips
> And sunshine in her hair.

Is that good poetry?"

"It's not poetry at all. It's the most awful hackneyed doggerel, and it's not about me." Carol felt unreasonably annoyed.

"I bet it is. I'll ask him when I give it back."

6

"I CANNOT adequately portray the effect of that light drizzle on the far hills," said Mr Sullivan.

"*You* can't?" said Vance. "You're the best artist among us."

"No, no, I can't," the old man went on. "Not the way I'd like to, not with that misty three-dimensional effect John Flavell achieves. That sense of distance is his particular gift. He say's it's not a trick, it's selection of observation. He's promised to take me out when the weather clears and show me what he means."

"I'm struggling with those hills too," said Josephine. "He tells me it's because I try to paint them exactly as I *think* I see them, and if I added imagination they'd actually look more realistic."

"Yes, that's his theme song," said Vance. "Make it *look* natural. He suggests you move trees around or leave out a hill or poke in a river — as though Nature didn't know her business. But you have to admit, his changes do improve a picture."

Rudolph objected. "Not always. He tends to put too much in his own paintings. He's an excellent artist, I know, but I think he adds features which would be better left out."

"Piffle!" said Myra Hurst. "You want things too simple. He knows what he's doing."

She and Rudolph were constantly arguing. If one made a statement, the other would almost certainly challenge it. Vance intervened before one of their prolonged wrangles could develop. "Flavell has the knack of putting his finger on your weak spot. Miss Pillington's useful in the basic stuff — mechanics and gimmicks. But it's Mrs Flavell who has the inspiration. She's a marvellous painter."

"She makes me feel a fool," said Carol. "She never smiles, and her remarks are often sarcastic."

"Good teacher for all that," said Myra. "Sneers at her husband rather than us. Don't know how the poor chap puts up with it."

"He takes no notice," said Vance. "He's too absorbed in his teaching and his painting to let it bother him. It'll be interesting to see who gets the breakfast tomorrow. The Ballins have gone into Brighton to see a new grandchild. They can hardly order Miss Pillington to do domestic duties, and Flavell's given his wrist such a wallop he can't use that hand at all."

"We may have to get our own. Who's giving the talk tonight?"

"Flavell. They all speak well, don't they?"

Everyone agreed. On one thing they were unanimous — the quality of the tuition and the excellence of the evening lectures, which were well presented, never long enough to be boring, and were usually illustrated by slides or demonstrations. According to Eva and

Myra, the same one was never given twice, so that students could come back year after year without fear of listening to a repetition.

"I wish they *would* give the same one twice," complained Susan that evening, as they were making supper in her room. "There's so much in them, and it's all so new to me I just can't take it all in. My mind's too tired at that hour."

"I don't think your abstract art is as relaxing as the other sort," said Carol. "Would you like to give it up and try landscape?"

"No, not now. It's not as easy as I used to think, and not as silly either. I bet if I saw *Emotion 25* again I'd like it better. There are rules, you know. You don't just dab colours on. Rudy says you paint the essence or spirit of a scene rather than the scene itself. You don't paint a picture of a man gazing at a sunset. You paint what the man *feels* when he gazes at a sunset. See?"

"No, I don't. Vance says Constable

called that stuff 'dreams of nonsense and abortions'. I don't know why you listen to that German criminal. He doesn't do abstract art himself and he's having you on. Buttering you up for some evil purpose of his own. Has he told you anything about his past yet?"

"No, why should he? Has Vance Mackay told you anything about his? He's always dancing attendance on you."

"I never ask him about his past. It doesn't concern me." Carol rather wished it did. Vance was a charming, entertaining young man, whom she liked well enough. But a smile from John Flavell could warm her right through — and he was neither available nor interested. Oh hell, why did she always like the *wrong* guys best?

"I gave that poem back to him," Susan was saying, "and I bet it *was* about you, because when I asked him if it was he got all flustered and said of course not, and tore it up. So I asked what he thought *your* hair was like, if that wasn't it, and — "

"And what?"

"He thought for a bit and then said it reminded him of the tangled wool on the head of a golliwog. Which proves he was covering up his feelings."

Carol was about to retort when there was a tap at the door. She opened it to find Josephine Satterley. "Can I speak to you a minute?" asked Josephine. "There's something I don't understand."

"*We're* not artists," said Carol. "I mean, we're not nearly as good as the others, or as you. We're not the ones to ask for help."

"It's not about art. It's only — "

"Come on in and sit down. We've just made some tea and there's a third cup, isn't there, Susan? Yes, here we are. Take milk?"

"Why don't you like painting?" said Susan, when they were sipping their tea. "We admire your work so much."

"It's the result of years of my father's

118

teaching and forced hard work on my part. I've no real natural talent."

"Mr Flavell says you have."

"Mr Flavell's a liar. Besides, I don't want to be an artist. I want to be a shorthand typist. But typists don't make a name in the world and they don't move in the best circles socially, so as far as my father's concerned that's out. Life can be hell, can't it?"

"Don't say that. Couldn't you ask your father to let you do a commercial course as a side-line?"

"I did. He won't. He's too ambitious for me. Honestly, life's hardly worth living sometimes, is it?"

"How old are you?" asked Carol.

"Twenty."

"Have you any money of your own?"

"Oh yes. I get a good allowance. It's not that."

"Then can't you use some of it to take a course? You're not a prisoner, are you? You could learn shorthand in the afternoons and buy yourself a typewriter to practise on at home. Or would your father ask where you'd been each day?"

"No, he's not interested. He just asks what I've *painted* each day."

"You could paint in the mornings," Carol continued.

Josephine was looking at her reflectively. "It's an idea."

"Think it over. In the meantime, get what you can out of your stay here. Paint something good to please your father, and the rest of the time just enjoy the surroundings and the company. They're a jolly decent crowd, aren't they?"

"Mrs Flavell's a bitch."

Carol did not comment. One must not encourage twenty-year-olds to voice the uncharitable sentiments one secretly harbours oneself.

"Maybe you're right," said Josephine. "If I took something home to please the old boy and told him I didn't keep the others?"

"I'd take them all home. You've done some lovely work."

"I don't want to talk about painting." Josephine frowned.

"Then let me get you some more tea." How young she is, thought Carol. Young and unhappy, and just a little spoilt. She must keep her chatting. "It was awful about Mr Flavell falling down the quarry, wasn't it?" she remarked.

"Yes. I saw him up there on the slope that morning, and I thought at the time it looked dangerous."

"You didn't see him fall?"

"No, it must have happened after I walked on. I went round the front to have another look at that huge chestnut by the parking area. Have you ever thought of painting it?"

"You see, you *are* interested in painting," said Carol. "Are you doing it?"

"I intended to then. I started a sketch of it, but then Mr Mackay came round the corner and I ducked inside so I wouldn't have to talk to him."

"Oh, Josephine! Why don't you like talking to people?"

121

"It's just the people *here* I don't like talking to. They're all artists, and I'm sick of artists. I see too many at home."

"Then what do you do in your spare time here?"

"Wander round the grounds mostly."

"Well, don't wander along the quarry head, will you? If Mr Flavell can fall down, it must be dangerous."

"I wouldn't go near that part. Anyway, I saw Mr Flavell putting a bolt on the gate up there tonight, just before the lecture."

"To keep us out? That's a pity, because that hilltop's the only place where you can see the sea, and you have to go through the fence to get a good view of it. There's really heaps of room the other side of the fence. You don't need to go over by the edge."

"He can't take the risk of anyone else falling," said Susan. "*He* didn't expect the ground to give way, and the same thing could happen to someone else just as easily. Wasn't that an interesting talk he gave tonight?"

"Rather," agreed Carol. "Didn't you think so, Josephine? *Oddities of artists*. I didn't know that Leonardo da Vinci wrote from right to left, or that William Blake and his wife caused a sensation by sitting naked in their garden reading Milton. Why not, anyway, if they wanted to? There's a certain freedom about artists. So cheer up, Josephine. Make painting a hobby, to please your father, and because you have talent, and do a commercial course on the side."

"That's not a bad idea." Josephine got up. "Thanks for the tea."

"What did you want to ask us about?"

"Oh — that — it doesn't matter. It was just — I may have been wrong. Good-night." She was smiling as she left the room.

"Poor kid," said Carol, as they washed the cups. "But why did she come to us, Sue? We were all talking in the common-room, and she could have asked then — whatever it was."

"I guess because she doesn't like artists and we're patently *not*. It must be hard having a famous father. Let's ask her to sit with us at breakfast tomorrow and get her talking some more. She's lonely, I think, and she could be quite nice when you get to know her."

Carol went back to her own room and got into bed, but she could not sleep for a while. There was something Josephine had said — something puzzling — something not quite right. What was it? The more she tried to identify it, the more elusive it became. It could not have registered clearly on her mind at the time, but had left only an after-impression, as when one walks through a familiar room and comes out knowing that a change has been made, a small article removed, added, or shifted, but memory will not specify which. It might become clear when they talked with Josephine at breakfast tomorrow.

7

BUT Josephine was not at breakfast the next morning. Neither were Eva or Mr Sullivan. This was not unusual. It had become a point of honour to be punctual at the studio, and if you slept in it was breakfast you sacrificed. Josephine had missed it several times before, though not, in her case, from over-sleeping, for she had been seen strolling about the grounds at that hour. Carol suspected she was paying attention to her figure.

Mrs Flavell had evidently cooked the breakfast herself, for she brought in the food, but she did not wait on the tables. The cereal, fruit, hot dishes, toast and coffee were all laid out on the sideboard for the students to help themselves.

The tutors were not in the studio at nine o'clock, and no set directions had been given. So Carol decided to start a picture of the open sea, with gulls swooping across. It was a trite subject, but she would do it all in muted greys and greens, trying to achieve the soft pale harmony of some of Josephine's paintings. Susan drew a distorted orange circle and coloured it in. The sun? No, it was more like the yolk of an egg. So she left an irregular white space around it and filled in the background with black. "I'm going to call it *Egg*," she told Carol.

Carol looked at it. "Are you?" she said. It was not a brilliant or helpful comment, but the only one she could think of. She began mixing viridian, burnt sienna and ultramarine together to make a base for her proposed cumulo-nimbus masses.

Josephine was still not in the studio by half-past nine. "Do you think she's slept in this time?" said Susan. "She's never been late for classes before."

"No, she's wandering round outside, feeling sorry for herself, and has lost track of the time. She doesn't care, that's the trouble. She's not interested and won't try."

"But she's entered for the Sanderson-Ebbings, isn't she, Eva?"

"Yes, her father put her name in, she says," Eva told them. "And she really is trying, in spite of what she says. Either she's afraid of that father of hers, or she wants to please him. She was asking me yesterday how to do hills in the distance. As if *I* would know! I ask you! Go to the experts, I told her. Don't pick on the worst painter in the room."

"The tutors are late too," Susan remarked. "Have they all slept in?"

There was a feeling of freedom with the tutors absent, and more chatter than usual. Myra and Rudolph had started to argue, as they so often did. Myra's voice was raised, loud and strident. " — then originality becomes worshipped as a god and they sacrifice all to it — beauty, harmony and even truth. If a thing flouts tradition, they

127

imagine it to be good. And the warped, childish, ugly results of their striving to be different are hung in galleries for the feeble-minded to admire because the catalogue tells them they should."

Then Rudolph's clear, precise tone: "It's those who cling to traditional values who betray an inability to think for themselves. The normal person identifies beauty according to his early training. At an impressionable age he's told that certain shapes, colours and arrangements are desirable, and he meekly accepts the dictum of his elders. 'Isn't Aunt Helen lovely!' 'Look at that pretty wallpaper!' Our European standards are not universal. An African child may be told to be proud of his cousin Pogobobo because she has the flattest, widest nose and the thickest lips in the village, 'and if you're a good girl and eat up all your collar-bones, you may grow up to be beautiful like her'."

Carol listened as she painted. Myra became heated at times. Rudolph's voice remained steady, decisive but unemotional. A spy or the head of a criminal organisation would have had to learn such control. Her distrust of the man was growing. What *could* Susan see in him? That grey was not quite what she wanted for the sky. She'd try viridian with rose madder.

Then John Flavell entered. He walked straight to the dais and rang the bell. Even before he spoke it was obvious that something was wrong. His face was drawn and for a moment he seemed unable to speak. Then the words jerked out, hoarsely, reluctantly. "I am very sorry to tell you — there has been a tragic accident. You probably saw an ambulance arrive — " He paused, bit his lip, and then, as if forcing himself to continue, went on, "Miss Satterley has been found at the foot of the quarry. She is — that is — her fall was fatal. Her neck is broken."

There was a hush in the room, that strange silence which is more intense than mere absence of conversation, the silence which is felt when a group of people is horrified into complete immobility. Flavell spoke again. "Comment would be superfluous, and moreover I feel unable — " His voice faltered and he stroked his forehead with his right hand as if to brush away a lingering nightmare. He made another effort. "Please continue with your work. That is the best thing to do. Miss Pillington will be with you shortly. You will excuse me. There are matters to attend to."

He left the room, walking uncertainly, as if not fully awake. For some moments no one spoke. Then Vance said, "What was she doing up at the quarry?"

"She often walked round during breakfast," said Myra. "And she wasn't happy with her distance effects. Good view from up there."

Miss Pillington arrived, and they continued to work. All painted mechanically, listlessly, trying without success to keep their minds on their colours and composition. Susan's *Egg* received no praise. Apparently a fellow called Miro had got in first, done much the same thing and called it *Disque Rouge*. It was now a recognised masterpiece, owned by a private collector in New York. "The plagiarism is quite unconscious," said Miss Pillington. "We all do it at times. You have at some time seen a reproduction, its excellence has impressed you, your unconscious has stored it up, and now it emerges as a seemingly original thought."

She passed on to Carol. "That is not the formation of the swell on an open sea, Miss Barton. The pattern is more lozenge shaped." Her voice was a little unsteady, and Carol noticed her hand shaking as she took up a brush to demonstrate.

A car was heard coming up the drive, and Stein went over to the window. "Police car," he said in answer to enquiring looks. No one commented.

The morning break was short. Mrs Ballins had just come back, and it was she who brought up the trolley in the lift, wheeled it a few feet into the room, and left again without a word. They went over to pour their own tea or coffee, avoiding looking at one another, as if fearing to see the distress and shock which must be showing on every face.

Lunch was a short meal, too, eaten in almost complete silence. Near the end of the meal someone asked Mrs Ballins about her trip to Brighton. Her face lightened briefly when she spoke of the baby — eight and a half pounds it was, and quite a head of dark hair — the dearest little soul — she didn't know how her daughter was going to manage, with three of them under school age. Suddenly everyone was intensely interested in the housekeeper's daughter's baby. Whom did it look like? Wasn't the father proud? She would be looking forward to her next week off between courses. Would Mr Ballins go with her? Then Mrs Ballins went back to the kitchen and conversation stopped again.

Mrs Flavell was present in the studio after lunch. She looked as usual, showing no signs of distress on her hard face. One student the less — it might have been a broken chair or lost laundry. The fees are paid in advance, thought Carol, so what's it to her? A bit of a nuisance, but a profit on the food. Then she told herself not to be uncharitable. You couldn't always tell a person's feelings by the expression on their face. Mrs Flavell passed from student to student, explaining, criticising, helping, advising, demonstrating, as on any other day. That didn't mean she was not inwardly upset. They were all trying to conceal their distress.

Mr Flavell made another appearance in the mid-afternoon. He looked more composed now. He spoke to them briefly. "I feel that I am myself partly responsible for the terrible tragedy this morning. I had reason to know that the ground was unsafe — " he glanced down at his left arm in its sling — "but I had not expected anyone else to go through the fence. I put a bolt on the gate last evening, but forgot to take a padlock up with me. That has now been rectified. We shall take no further risks. From now on the area above the quarry beyond the fence is strictly out of bounds. If the padlocked gate is not sufficient deterrent — anyone found climbing through the fence will be at once asked to leave." He walked out of the room without looking at them again. Mrs Flavell followed him out.

"That's telling us," said Myra.

"Can you blame him?" asked Rudolph.

"If he'd put a padlock on it wouldn't have happened. No wonder he's upset."

"It's not his fault," Carol protested. "He can't be expected to go round blocking off every danger spot, as though it were a kindergarten he's running. And Josephine could still have climbed through the fence or over the gate."

Vance agreed. "If you want to torture yourself, you can always think up a way you could have prevented an accident. Having the fence there was adequate protection. It's this side of the boundary, isn't it, Miss Pillington?"

"Yes. It was erected only a few years ago and put several yards this side of the boundary, they told me, in order to give the quarry workers more freedom at the top. A few perches were nothing to the Flavells."

Now that the subject had been broached and both Flavells were out of the room, it became easier to talk about the accident. Miss Pillington was asked for more details, and told what she knew. Miss Satterley had been found by Mrs Flavell, shortly before half-past eight that morning. Mrs Flavell had gone out to collect a collapsible table which had been left in the grounds, and had seen the body as she walked behind the house. She had gone straight over to investigate (she *would*, thought Carol) and then returned to fetch her husband. The clay above the quarry had apparently given way, for clumps had been found near the body. An inquest would be held.

They packed up soon after that. Miss Pillington suggested it, and all agreed.

8

THE sun was shining again next morning, but the atmosphere among the students was heavy and dull, most of them experiencing that sense of unreality which proximity to sudden death so often brings. It couldn't be true — but it was.

Carol and Susan sat with Eva and Myra at breakfast. The conversation was desultory and stilted, as though each feared to hurt by mentioning the subject uppermost in her mind. Myra never talked much, except when engaged in an argument of her own choosing. But Carol was surprised at Eva's restraint. It did not seem true to type that her bubbling inconsequential chatter could be turned off at will through good taste. But then other things about Eva were not true to type. One would expect her to take pleasure in recounting past illnesses, the unusual features of her symptoms while she was at death's door, and the amazement of the doctors at her recovery. 'You have only yourself to thank, Miss Tritt. It was your determination, your courage, your refusal to give in. Any other woman.' Or she should be describing her exceptionally gifted little nephews and nieces. 'The teacher said she'd never *known* a child learn so quickly.' Yet Eva did none of that. Her conversation was mainly on topical, general subjects, and among the babbling were interspersed a few shrewd and penetrating remarks. Moreover she was kind, genuinely kind. She was talking now to Mrs Ballins.

"I'd be grateful for a drive out of the place after class, so you'd be doing me a favour."

"That's really very kind of you, Miss Tritt. I'll ask Albert. You've been so good, and I must admit it's so much quicker and easier than doing it by mail. Saves all that paper-work, and

I'm afraid that sort of thing is not our strong point."

"Well, cooking is," said Eva. "This plaice is done to perfection."

When they reported to the studio at nine o'clock, Miss Pillington announced that they would be painting indoors again, in spite of the sunshine. No reason was given. Exercises were set, but they were optional, and most worked on unfinished canvases. No one talked much. Once it was remarked that strangers were wandering about the grounds, and a few went to the windows for a closer look.

During the morning they were called out one by one.

"They want you next," said Myra to Susan. "It's in the library — that's the room opening off the hall opposite the common-room."

"Who are they? What do they want?"

"Police. Doesn't take long. Just questions about Josephine."

The library was a lovely old room.

Apart from the installation of wall-heaters, it had not been modernised, and with lines of bookshelves, leather-covered chairs and heavily framed old oil paintings, it had an air of old-world graciousness which the common-room lacked. Two men were sitting at a table. They rose politely as Susan entered and gestured her to a chair in front of the table. They did not introduce themselves. Both had paper and pens before them, and one began writing as she spoke. She thought irrelevantly that the pressure of his ball-point through the thin pad might indent the beautifully polished surface of the walnut table.

"Miss Meadows?" said the one facing her, as he consulted a list before him. "Is this your correct name and address?" He pushed over a paper, and Susan nodded. "I'm sorry to interrupt your work, but there are a few routine questions we are obliged to ask in connection with yesterday's tragedy. I hope you don't mind?"

"Of course not." Would it make any difference if she did?

"How well did you know Miss Satterley?"

"I hadn't met her before I came here, and she was rather reserved."

"Did she appear to you to be happy?"

Susan considered a moment before replying. "I think so. I don't really know. She wasn't as interested in the course as the rest of us."

"Did she seem depressed — worried — under strain?"

"N-no. I don't think so."

"When did you see her last?"

"The night before she — before it happened. She came to my room where my friend and I were having a cup of tea before going to bed."

"Your friend?"

"Carol Barton."

He looked at his list. "Ah yes. And what did she want?"

Susan hesitated. Josephine had wanted to ask them something, and she had not done so. But then she said it didn't matter, so it couldn't have been important. The men were looking at her, waiting. "Nothing special," she said. "Just a friendly visit."

"Did you have the impression during the visit that she was unhappy or worried?"

"When she left she seemed cheerful. She was smiling."

"Then there is nothing you know of which might indicate a desire to take her own life?"

Susan stared. "Oh, she *didn't*. The bank gave way — didn't it?"

"Probably, but we have to consider every possibility. So would you answer the question please? Take your time. Think first. Had anything happened to upset her? Do you know if she received a disturbing letter or phone call? Did she at any time show signs of undue distress or despondency, or of having a personal problem?"

"Oh, *no*."

He stared at her for a few seconds,

hard, searchingly, and then said, "Thank you, Miss Meadows. That will be all. Would you be good enough to ask — let me see — Mr Sullivan, if he could spare us a few minutes?"

Susan returned to the studio a little uneasy about her answers to the questions. Josephine *had* been worried when she came to see them that evening. But not enough to kill herself, to throw herself off a cliff. Oh no, it wasn't possible. Yet she was despondent, fed up — well, Carol could tell them so if she thought fit, when it was her turn to be interviewed.

"But *was* she distressed?" asked Carol when they discussed it. "I don't want to put them wrong."

"I said she wasn't unhappy. And that isn't true. She was."

"But not enough to jump over a cliff. Even if she did want to commit suicide there are easier ways than that." But she kept on thinking about it when Susan went back to her desk. It wasn't impossible. What had Josephine said?

'Life's hardly worth living.' Suppose she had really meant it? Suppose she had been standing at the quarry-head, gazing out at the horizon, and a sudden fit of despair came over her — one step forward and she could end it all. Is that how it happened? Yet many people made such impulsive statements at times, and they didn't mean anything. It was like saying 'I could kill that baker. He's left me stale bread' or 'I'd give my right arm to sing like you'. Just a way of speaking. Wasn't it that with Josephine?

She was still turning this over in her mind when John Flavell came to see her work. His face was grim, but he forced a smile. "How are those grasses coming along? I think you could afford more emphasis just here. May I?" He picked up a brush and with a few quick strokes livened the foreground.

"How different that looks! But now I can't say I painted it."

"You're more honest than most people. You don't realise how many famous paintings hung in galleries contain features copied from the works of other artists. It's considered allowable."

"But that's cheating."

"It's recognition of what is good. But I wouldn't have you do it. Stay the way you are, Carol. Straight and honest."

"John, to what extent should one be honest? It's my turn soon to be interviewed and I'm not sure what to say. Do they really suspect Josephine of taking her own life?"

"I doubt it. It's just part of the routine to consider that possibility. In the event of any fatal accident, they have a certain procedure."

"They're asking everyone if she was depressed. Sue said no, but Josephine *was* depressed. She said she didn't want to paint."

"Don't be deceived by her manner. She was really anxious to please her father, whatever she may have told you, and she had a good chance for the Sanderson-Ebbings grant. I had a long talk with her a few days ago, and she was surprised at the progress which I could point out she'd made. She believed me. I've no doubt of that. She knew, as you know, that I don't praise falsely. That helps no one. She was in no state to commit suicide. I can assure you of that."

"Then what was she doing up at the quarry top?"

Flavell ran a hand over his brow. "That's what I keep asking myself, followed closely by the question, am I responsible for her death? She wasn't satisfied with her way of indicating distance. I told her to observe more closely, to study the patterns in the colours of the sea as it faded towards the horizon, and the effect these colours had on the aspect of the far hills. I wonder — did she go up that morning because I'd advised her to?"

Carol saw the pain in his eyes, and it seemed to hurt her physically in sympathy. "Of course it wasn't your fault," she said emphatically. "She

146

didn't have painting things with her, did she?"

"A notebook and soft pencil."

"But we all carry those. You told us to. It doesn't mean that she went up to sketch. She used to wander all over the place, just walking."

"If only I had remembered to take a padlock up when I put a bolt on the gate! Or if I hadn't been too lazy to go back and fetch one!"

"John, you can't blame yourself. The gate was bolted, and she'd have had to open it to go through. Everyone knew you'd fallen. Did she fall from the same place?"

"No, she wasn't so lucky. She fell from the middle, where there is more or less a straight drop."

"Then perhaps it *was* suicide. She said 'Life's hardly worth living at times'. Shouldn't I tell the police that?"

"She wouldn't have meant it, so what would be the purpose in repeating it? There are two possible verdicts for the coroner's court — accidental death or suicide. Her family are suffering enough from her loss without the added stigma of suicide. Any hint of that would double their worry and distress. They may even imagine that through forcing her to take this course they had driven her to end her life. God, I know what it is to be haunted by some responsibility in the death of that young girl — at the beginning of her life — so much before her — " He stopped, seeming unable to go on.

"But is it honest to say nothing about what she said?"

"It's wiser and kinder. Now *why* have you put burnt umber in the foliage of that willow?"

"How did you know I did?"

The conversation became technical. They were still discussing the composition of various greens when Carol was summoned. Her interview was brief. Yes, that was her name and address. No, Miss Satterley had shown no signs of undue depression, she knew of no reason why she should take her own life —

Dinner was a quiet meal. Two of the three tables had been placed together to form a larger one, an attempt perhaps to make the gap seem less obvious. What conversation there was related mainly to art. Vance and Rudolph started a discussion on the respective merits of the early and late works of Juan Gris. Myra threw in a few comments from the next table, but it did not develop into a spirited dispute, as it might have done two days before. Eva commented once on the lemon dress Carol was wearing. "Such a lovely colour for you, my dear. It sets off your hair."

"Which I hear resembles the wool on a golliwog," said Carol, glaring at Vance.

"I like golliwogs," said Vance mildly. "I had a favourite one as a child." He grinned at her. It was hard to remain annoyed with Vance. His cheerful manner and smiling eyes had made him popular with the group, and even against her will Carol felt flattered by his attentions.

Only once that evening was the tragedy mentioned. During coffee someone remarked on the increasing difficulty of crawling out of bed in time for breakfast. "We're all becoming lazy."

Mr Sullivan agreed. "That is true. It has passed through my mind, if I had made a little more effort yesterday, would it have averted the terrible accident?"

"How could it? What do you mean?"

"Just by being in a certain place at a certain time one can vitally affect another's life. John wanted to take me up to the quarry head that morning to show me his theory of interpreting distance. If we had been there — " The old man's gentle face took on a look of distress.

"You didn't go?"

"No, I was too lazy. John was quite insistent, but I really couldn't. When my arthritis plays up — as it does in this changeable weather — climbing a hill is a physical agony which is not worth the achievement. But if I had consented — if we had been there — "

"Stop it," said Vance. "Don't *you* start blaming yourself. Flavell's already taking the responsibility. It's no one's fault."

"Of course not," agreed Rudolph. "You might say that every event in the world is in some way dependent on the whereabouts of the population individually. Just by walking down a street at a certain hour it could be possible indirectly to cause the death of another being."

"Or save it," said Mr Sullivan unhappily.

"Stupid to think like that," said Myra. "Change the subject."

"Yes, please do," begged Carol. "Can any of you tell me why Rossetti painted all his women with advanced goitre? Those prints Miss Pillington showed us the other night — "

"Not the thyroid," broke in Myra. "Have a closer look. He gave prominence to the hyoid bone and enlarged the sterno-mastoid. The female throat fascinated him."

"*One* throat," contradicted Rudolph. "Eleanor Siddal was his model for years and it's apparent she had an unusually well-developed — "

"Mission accomplished," whispered Carol as she pulled Susan away. "They'll argue over that all night. Let's get ourselves more coffee." They took their refilled cups to another corner of the room while the others discussed the Pre-Raphaelites. A few days ago they would have listened eagerly and taken part as far as their limited knowledge of art history allowed. Tonight the effort would have been too much strain.

For the first time, too, the evening lecture dragged. It was excellently prepared as usual, a talk by Miss Pillington on the sculptures of Constantin Brancusi. But Carol found herself fidgeting. When the last exhibit was shown — a photograph of Brancusi's *Fish* — Miss Pillington's words whirled confusedly in her ears. " — and I can best conclude with an analysis of its worth by Schwartz. I quote, 'The natural reference persists as internal organic energy and the anti-natural is conjured up by the authority of the conceptualised image and the actuality of the stone. In other words, the subject's visible attributes disappear, an inner force is activated, a highly charged metaphor is created.'" Which must mean *something*, thought Carol, but it seemed a funny way to talk about what looked to her like an oval paving-stone mounted on a stick. She would never be an artist.

"But we weren't the only ones yawning," she remarked to Susan later. "I guess no one could keep their mind on Brancusi. Sue, how *could* Josephine fall? I can understand John falling, down in those bushes where you can't see the edge, but the centre's

153

clear. Why would she go and stand near enough to tumble over? Do you think it could have been suicide?"

"I suppose it's possible. She was droopy and fed up with painting, but when she left us that night I thought she'd cheered up. If it *was* suicide, I hope no one ever knows."

"That's what John says. It's terrible for him. He looks so — broken, somehow, shattered."

"He feels responsible. Perhaps he is."

"How can he be?" said Carol quickly, too quickly. "It wasn't his fault." She could not forget his face as he stood on the dais that morning — almost frozen into a mask of shock and dismay. She felt for him with an intensity which startled her. I'm not really falling for him, she assured herself. A married man, seven or eight years older than herself. If that was Nature's dirty little scheme for her, she'd fight it all the way. Of course one felt pity for him — liking — gratitude — that's all it was.

154

9

AN inquest was held two days later in the Little Dorley village hall. Mr and Mrs Flavell had notice to attend. A verdict of accidental death was returned, and the coroner stressed the fact that no blame attached to any person or persons.

Classes continued. All applied themselves hard, hoping that concentration on their work would help rid them of other preoccupations. They painted indoors again, but there was no question of going up the hill. It was known that Mr Flavell had added a padlock to the bolt on the gate, and the key to the lock was kept in his own quarters. He spoke of it to Carol one day. "Of course it wouldn't keep out anyone who was determined to go to the other side of the fence. One could climb through the wires or over the gate. But it'll serve as a warning, a reminder. I'm thinking of putting the whole hilltop out of bounds."

"That would be a pity."

"It would be only temporary. We're going to have the fence shifted soon. Its present position is well this side of the boundary. My wife and I will have a good look at the ground to see how far it's undermined. We may employ an engineer to give his opinion, as we don't want to take any chances. Then we'll have the fence moved as near to the edge as possible within the bounds of absolute safety, and no one need go past it for a view."

"Was it very awful at the inquest?"

"No, the coroner was sympathetic. I blame myself bitterly, as you know, but he assured me that no one else does."

"Of course not. Try to put it out of your mind, John."

He smiled. "I certainly shouldn't be reminding you of it, but you're so easy to talk to, somehow. Try to keep your own thoughts on painting."

"Yes, we're more than half-way through the course already. I must make the most of the time that's left."

"I hope the end of the course won't mean the end of our — er — association. I'll be pleased to help you any time." He seemed a little embarrassed, and went on in a business-like, matter-of-fact tone, "Now, look at the scene in front of you — to the right there, towards the bird-bath. Half close your eyes, and tell me, where would you place the boundaries for a picture? What would you leave out? Would you put anything in? Shift any features? What will your focal point be?"

"Let me see." Carol settled eagerly to rearranging the disposition of the orchard. She was pleased with her progress lately. She would never be a great artist, but she had developed an understanding and improved vision. She could turn out a passably competent landscape sketch and she could look with a more critical eye at others' pictures.

Susan, too, attacked her work with enthusiasm, but was still surprised that Miss Pillington should praise it. "Don't let on," she said to Carol, "but I don't really think what she thinks I think."

"What does she think you think?"

"In this instance, that two widely divergent experiences are being dramatically integrated by that series of green broken lines."

Carol laughed. "You're certainly getting the jargon off pat."

"Yesterday I was awfully hungry and drew three chocolate bars, different shades of brown. She said it was reminiscent of George Braque's *clarinet*. She buzzed off and got me a photo of it."

"What, more plagiarism?"

"No, not this time. She seemed to think we'd both hit on the same brilliant image. She was pleased with me. How do you like this one?" Susan held up another sheet of paper. "Isn't it nice? I've named it *Memory at a Sundial*. You see that little black square? Miss Pillington says that's the key to the whole effect. Here, I cover the square with my finger. See the difference?"

"Yes. You've covered a little black square with a green, red and blue finger."

"When I cover it the whole concept changes. Miss Pillington says so. The meaning is gone."

"Has it? That's very impressive, Sue. What made you think of creating the significant black square?"

"I spilt a drop of milk there and tried to hide it."

"Oh. Is that — finished?"

"Of course it is. You should be able to tell. Moving, isn't it?"

"Not particularly. What are you going to do next?"

"Rudy thinks I ought to try some pop art. You know, mundane symbolic things like Richard Smith's *Cash Register* or

Alex Hay's *Posting Label*, only not realistic as they do them. Make a pattern from the same type of subject matter, he suggests, to show the underlying design in the apparent ugliness of the commercial world. What are you going to do next?"

"I want to paint a good seascape. Sea's awfully difficult. The beastly stuff *moves* all the time. Mrs Flavell does some marvellous sea paintings. I go and study those hung along the stairs, but it doesn't really help. I think I'll go up to the quarry top before dinner today, just to sit and stare at the sea and try to form my own idea on how to paint it. I can take notes of the streaks and colours and how the different depths show."

"Carol, you won't go near the — "

"Of course not. We're not allowed through the gate now, anyway. You can see the sea a bit from this side of the fence, on the top of the plateau. Not such a good view, but good enough for me, I think."

"Aren't you playing table tennis with Vance?"

"No. He's doing some work on his car. It's not running to his liking. He's a bit of a mechanic, I think."

"Then I'll come with you. Rudy has to go to the village."

"Oh, good." Susan usually went for a walk before dinner with Stein. If Carol was asked to accompany them she always had convincing reasons for doing something else. She was still prejudiced against Stein, but at least he had taken Sue's mind off her faithless Jim, and to that extent was useful. He was certainly a good artist. His paintings were usually quick studies, bold and masterful, with an element of design. He favoured strong outlines, and clear colours, and the effect was striking. But he remained evasive concerning his past. Every time Carol attempted to question him on it he avoided a direct answer, or gave one which told little. His German accent came and went with suspicious irregularity.

When they had showered and changed after class, they climbed up the wooded slope to the flat clearing at the top of the quarry, with sketch-books and pencils. A strong bolt had been fixed to the gate and a large padlock attached.

"It *would* be a deterrent," said Carol. "John was right."

"But you can hardly see the sea at all from this side of the fence. Josephine would have had to go through."

"No, you can't see as much as I thought. But, Sue, there's lots of room the other side. I can't understand why she went near enough to the edge to fall. It was different with John. He was at the far end, among those bushes, and some are overhanging so that you can't see the edge."

"He was lucky, because it's not a straight drop there. He would have rolled down that slope and landed on that flat bit. I suppose he was hunting for a new angle of view. He must get sick of painting the same old scenes over and over for clients.

Josephine could have been doing the same — hunting for the best view, inching forward trying to see what the sea was like nearer the shore, whether she could sight some rocks. Only she was nearer the middle of the curve and then the ground gave. Oh, don't let's talk about it!"

"No. Aren't the colours beautiful, and the clouds? Wouldn't you like to switch to water-colour so you could paint it?"

"I *can* paint it. I can analyse it into geometric forms and colour patterns."

"Hmm."

"You don't understand," said Susan smugly. "Your conception is limited. Rudy says — "

"Look, here's John," interrupted Carol.

Flavell was climbing up through the trees towards them. "What are you doing here?" he demanded when he reached the plateau. "You have no silly idea of climbing through that fence?"

His tone was angry, and Carol

rebelled. "Of course we haven't. You told us it was out of bounds. You treat us like school-children."

He appeared about to retort curtly, and then visibly relaxed. "You're right. I'm sorry. It's just that — I can't understand how Miss Satterley *could* have fallen."

"And you're afraid of another accident?"

"There'll be no more such accidents," he said grimly. "As you see, I've padlocked the gate so that no wandering hiker can leave it open. Ballins has orders to watch for anyone coming up to the quarry head. That's how I knew you were here. Now go back both of you and don't come again. Please," he added as an afterthought. Then he looked directly at Carol and said, "I don't want to be dictatorial, but I don't want you to take any risk at all." Was there a slight emphasis on the 'you'? Carol watched him as he turned abruptly and walked down the hill, without waiting for them to accompany him.

They followed more slowly. "I wish he wouldn't blame himself so," said Carol. "It's really bugging him. I've never seen him so angry.

Vance and Rudolph were outside the front door, sitting on the stone animals. Vance was flushed and breathing hard, as if he had been running.

"Have you finished your car?" Carol asked him.

"Car? Oh yes. I found the trouble."

"Ought you to sit on those pussy-cats?" asked Susan. "They might crumble under your weight."

"They're cheetahs," Rudolph told her, "and quite sturdy still."

"How do you know they're not panthers, or leopards?"

"They have a smaller head, longer legs, and small rounded ears, see? I must ask John how old they are. The style of their carving is remarkably similar to that of the marble figure by the summer-house. I suspect that the same artist did them."

"How can you tell?"

"Look at the treatment of the muscles. Come and see the one by the summer-house, and I'll explain what I mean."

"Don't you have to go to the village?"

"Tomorrow will do. Come on. Er — Carol?"

"No, thank you."

"I'll show her who's boss at billiards," said Vance. "On your way, golliwog."

"I beat him at table tennis yesterday," Carol explained. "I was so cross at being called that, it gave me oodles of adrenalin."

"It wasn't that at all. She didn't play fair. She wore that slinky blue dress, and I couldn't keep my eye on the ball."

Susan and Rudolph strolled slowly round the back of the house and down through the trees. Susan kept looking over to her right, where the quarry was. "Every time I see the quarry I think of that poor girl. And there's nowhere in the grounds from which you can't see it. It spoils the whole landscape."

"No it doesn't. It has something of its own, something which contrasts with the natural beauty of the trees and the lake, but is nonetheless worth study. Come over to the fence for a minute, and I'll show you what I mean."

They walked towards the right, where the fence came down the hill, skirting the side of the quarry. "Don't think of Josephine or of accidents," Stein said. "Just look at the quarry itself."

"Why don't they work it now? There's lots of metal left."

"They'll be back soon, I guess, with their front-end loaders and their trucks and their shovels. The crusher is still there. Now take a good look. Study the shape of the whole, then the rocks at the bottom, and the focal point of the crusher. Try to find a pattern, a man-made pattern, symbolising destruction if you like, or progress, or commercial greed. Put your own interpretation on it. Or even simply a design with no meaning, but pleasing to look at. Half close your eyes and look for a pattern. It's there if you can find it."

Susan screwed up her eyes. "I see what you mean. One could strengthen the light on the slopes, then darken the shadows of the rocks at the bottom, and that long one of the crusher — would you leave it out, or emphasise that old barrow? And that dark mass beside it? What is it? It looks like a bundle of clothes."

"Yes. Perhaps workmen have been here. They may be going to start up again soon. Come along the fence a bit. You can see more clearly further down."

They walked down beside the fence until they were nearer the wide bottom curve of the quarry. Suddenly Stein stopped. He put his hand on Susan's arm. "Stop, Susan. Don't come any closer. Just wait there for me." He squeezed through the wires of the fence and ran quickly across the stones. Susan watched, puzzled. Then she climbed through the fence herself. She was not used to obeying orders given by young men.

He was bending over the bundle of clothes when she came up to him, turning it over. Then he saw her, rose, and stood between it and her. His face was grim. "Don't look, Susan. It's — there's been another accident."

"What — who — "

"It's Mrs Flavell. And she's dead."

10

JOHN FLAVELL stood on the dais, regarding his students. What he had to say would already have been told them by Miss Pillington, but he considered it his responsibility to make an official announcement. He must get it over with. He had slept little and was very tired. His hands were trembling slightly, so he clasped them tightly together. He spoke slowly and dully. "Thank you all for your expressions of sympathy. I asked you to assemble here this morning to tell you that the course is terminated. I'm sorry, but I think you will understand that I cannot carry on with this session. Your second and third week's fee will be refunded in full. In view of personal arrangements already made, it may not be convenient for some of you who travelled a long way to leave immediately. You are welcome to stay until it suits you to return home. Mrs Ballins will continue to cook meals and assist in any way she can. The hilltop is strictly out of bounds."

He stopped. There was nothing else worth saying. He looked briefly round them. A good lot this time — Miss Tritt, faithful Miss Tritt, kind old soul — Sullivan, quite an honour having him; those two young gate-crashers, the nerve of them! They'd never held a brush in their lives. Carol looked drawn, pale, shocked, all the spirit knocked out of her. He wished it didn't hurt him so much to see her like that. He stepped down and left the studio, shoulders bent.

Carol and Susan gathered up their materials and walked down to their rooms to pack. "We can get away before lunch," said Carol, "and stop at a pub for a meal. Did you sleep last night?"

"No, I kept seeing *her*. That bundle. She was wearing a dark blue dress, not a smock, and it looked like a heap of dark clothes." Susan shuddered. "How would it happen? Why did she go through the gate?"

"John said yesterday that they were both worried about the state of the ground and were going to examine it, then shift the fence nearer the quarry edge so students could get a better view of the sea without going through. There was lots of room. It was just a matter of how far over it was safe to move it."

"Yes, there *was* lots of room beyond the fence. And she was so practical. Not the sort to take risks. Not like Mr Flavell himself, or Vance or Eva — or us, perhaps. So why did she go so close? *She* wouldn't have jumped over, would she?"

"No. She disliked others, but she seemed satisfied enough with herself. And she was in line for that award thing, which seems worth having."

"She wasn't on friendly terms with her husband."

"But he was nice to her. You don't

throw yourself over a cliff because you disapprove of another person." Carol turned to go into her room, and saw Mrs Ballins coming up the stairs. She looked tired and worried.

"Oh, there you are, girls. I thought you might have come up. I'm sorry, but I've been asked to let everyone know that the police are here again, and they don't want anyone to leave just yet. They want you all in the common-room at eleven."

"Are they the same two policemen who came last time?"

"No, I think they're from the city. Dozens of them. They're all over the grounds and the house." She passed a hand over her forehead. "It's bad enough without all this as well."

"Have you had accidents at the quarry before?"

"Not as long as we've been here, and I've never heard of any happening before. It was the heavy rain, it seems. I'm sure I don't know."

"It must be terrible for Mr Flavell."

"Oh, it is, Miss Barton. I'm ever so sorry for him. And such a nice gentleman, it doesn't seem fair." She passed on to knock at the next door.

Susan sighed. "More questions, I suppose, as to whether the deceased was depressed, what was her state of mind, and so on. Carol, I feel so awful because I *don't* feel so awful. Not like when Josephine — "

"I know just what you mean. If we'd had to choose any single person out of the household — Well, we'll be out of it soon."

The assembly in the common-room at eleven was hushed and subdued. Carol thought Vance had a weary, rather than tragic, look. Not Rudolph, though. His face was set, grim, menacing. Vance saw them come in and walked over to sit down wordlessly by Carol, as if to protect her.

Eva was by herself, strangely composed. Mr Sullivan was beside Myra, who was leaning towards him, talking earnestly, as if to reassure.

Then Miss Pillington entered with two strangers. They did not sit. One of them spoke. "I am Chief Detective-Inspector Lang. And this is Detective-Inspector Paterson. Thank you for coming so promptly. You will realise that in circumstances such as these there is a certain routine procedure to be followed. I know your course has been cancelled, but I understand that you would normally be staying here until Sunday week. I'm afraid I must ask all of you not to leave until a few preliminary enquiries are made. We shall try to be brief and to delay you as little as possible, but we would like a statement from each of you. I must make it clear that you are none of you obliged to answer any questions put to you, but your co-operation would be appreciated." He left the room with his assistant.

"What does that mean?" said Vance. "Please would we answer questions but we don't have to? They surely don't think *she* jumped over deliberately, do they? Do you know, Miss Pillington?"

"I don't know what they think," she told him. "They're not talkative. They were a long time last night with Mr Flavell and then again this morning, and now there seem to be men all over the place, some in uniform and some not. They've been over to the quarry taking photographs and there are constables roaming about the grounds."

"They had you in for a long time last night, Mr Stein," said Eva.

Stein frowned. "I had to make a statement and sign it."

"Why did she go up there? How did she get through the gate?"

Miss Pillington answered. "She had access to the key. The police found the gate open and the key in the padlock. They told me that much."

"But why did she go at all?" asked Susan.

"She was very puzzled at Miss Satterley's falling. She kept saying she didn't understand. I suppose she went up to see for herself what the ground was like and how far they could shift the fence."

"Miss Meadows!" Mrs Ballins had appeared at Susan's side. "The inspector says could you spare him a few minutes please? In the library."

Both inspectors were in the library and rose as she entered. A constable sitting at a small table ignored her and continued writing.

"Please sit down, Miss Meadows," said Inspector Lang. He was a large, grey-haired man with a deceptive air of fatherly kindness. "Thank you for coming. We shan't keep you long. There are, you understand, routine enquiries — "

"Of course." Susan sat down. She seemed to have heard it all before.

"Mr Stein has made a full statement concerning the finding of the body. It must have been a dreadful shock to you. I understand you did not touch the body yourself?"

"No, I didn't go right up to it. He stopped me."

"Quite so. Then you went for help while Mr Stein stayed?"

"Yes. I met Mr Ballins and told him, and he — sort of took over." She had been so grateful to Ballins, who had gone in to break the news to John Flavell.

"Yes. Now there are just a few questions, Miss Meadows — "

Here we go again. Well, she'd been prepared for that. Whether she considered Mrs Flavell could have taken her own life, what state of mind was she in — Susan had decided she would simply say she was incapable of forming any opinion. The constable had his notebook poised, she noticed.

"You understand you are not obliged to answer any questions?"

"Why shouldn't I? Why do you say that?"

"I want to make it quite clear. You may refuse to answer any question I ask. Now, you're doing pastel work, I'm told?"

"Yes."

"Oil based?"

"No, just chalk."

"Your pastels were not in the studio this morning."

Why were they hunting for her pastels in the studio? "No, it's just a small box and I usually carry them in my handbag."

"Are they in the bag now?" He nodded towards it.

"Yes." She opened her bag and handed the inspector the box of pastels. Both men seemed inordinately interested in the contents. One smeared the back of his hand with blue chalk, and rubbed the colour thoughtfully with his forefinger. "This is all you use?"

"Yes."

"Have you tried oils at all during the course?"

"No, but I spent the first day with water-colour."

He handed the box back to her. "Messy things, aren't they?"

"Very." Susan looked at him, surprised. Why the small-talk?

179

"Now, Miss Meadows, what were you doing yesterday afternoon?"

"We were all outside painting. In the orchard at the side of the house."

"All? Was everyone present? Including the tutors? Mrs Flavell?"

"I think so. Mrs Flavell came to me at least three times."

"When the class finished, what did you do then?"

"We went up to our rooms to shower and change. Carol Barton and I."

"How long were you in your room?"

"I don't know. I get messy and I like to shower straight away after classes and change my dress. About twenty minutes? Half an hour? I'm sorry, I can't be sure."

"And what did you do next?"

"I went down with Carol."

"Had she been in her room while you were changing?"

"Of course."

"How do you know?"

"Well, I — well, she *was*." They were staring at her, waiting. "I heard her in the bathroom after me," Susan remembered. "It's between our rooms."

"You stopped painting, I understand, at four-thirty. It would take you some time to pack up and come to your room. At what time would you say you and Miss Barton went downstairs after changing?"

"I've no idea. I didn't look at the time. After five, I guess."

They looked a little annoyed. How could she be expected to remember how long it took to shower and change? You didn't time yourself.

"And where did you go then?"

"We went up through the trees towards the plateau at the top of the hill. Carol wanted to look at the sea."

"Whom did you see on the way there?"

Susan thought. "Mr Ballins was in the kitchen garden, I think. And we passed Miss Hurst. She was going down the valley. No one else."

"How long did you stay at the top of the hill?"

"I don't know. Not very long, because Mr Flavell came up after us and ordered us down. So we went."

"With Mr Flavell?"

"No, he went first. We followed a few minutes later."

"Did you see Mr Flavell as you went down?"

"No, the trees are thick on the hill. Besides, we were talking."

"Did you see anyone at all as you went down? Where did you go?"

"We went back to the house and we didn't see anyone until we got there. Mr Mackay and Mr Stein were in front, sitting on the cats."

"I beg your pardon?"

"On the stone carvings on the porch."

"What time was that?"

"I don't know."

The questions continued. How long had she spoken with the men, when did they leave, where did she and Mr Stein go, at what time, how far had they walked before they turned towards the fence, where was she standing, was anyone else in sight? Again the details about finding the body, informing Mr Ballins. It went on and on. At last the inspector said, "Thank you, Miss Meadows. I'm sorry to have had to recall all this to your mind. I shall have a statement typed out and later ask you to sign it if you consider it correct. I don't think it will be necessary for you to attend the inquest." He nodded to the constable, who rose and opened the door for her.

She was faced with more questions when she returned to the common-room. It was noticeable that there was not the same reticence about this tragedy as about the last. Perhaps no one felt the loss so much. "What did they ask you?" — "Do they think she committed suicide?"

"They asked me all about drawing in pastels," said Susan.

"Perhaps they want to pick up some tips while they're here. Police with unfulfilled ambitions. Is that all they asked about?"

"No. They wanted details of what I did all yesterday afternoon. And about finding the body. That was horrid."

Rudolph said firmly, "That's enough. Don't talk about it."

"No. We were going down to the lake, Rudy?"

"I'm sorry, Susan. It seems I have to stick around for a bit."

Mrs Ballins entered. "The inspector would like you now, Miss Hurst."

Lunch was served at the usual time. Miss Pillington came in during it to make an announcement. "I've been asked to tell you that the studio will be open, and you're welcome to use it while you're here. There will be no further lessons, but there's no hurry to leave. You're invited to stay on a few days as Mr Flavell's guests if you wish."

"Decent of him," grunted Myra.

"Oh, isn't that *kind*!" said Eva. "I shall certainly stay. I mean to do a painting of the dove-cots — really, so *good* of him to think of it."

One by one during the day the students were called to the library. Each had the same to report. "He asked me whether I do oils, and where I keep them." — "They wanted to know how many days I'd been on acrylics." — "Did I do only water-colour?" — "What's the matter with them? What's all that got to do with falling over a bank?" All had been closely questioned over their movements of the afternoon before. Rudolph Stein was kept a particularly long time, and recalled twice. Perhaps he was on their files and had been recognised, thought Carol. She'd never trusted him. Oh Sue, why do you spend so much time with him? Though I can hardly blame you, when I've fallen for the wrong guy too.

Whereas Josephine's death had produced reserve among the students, the latest tragedy seemed to bring them closer together. They discussed it freely.

Miss Tritt was back to her chatty self, and had quite decided what had caused the accident. "She went up to examine the ground, moved too close to the edge, and the clay gave way."

"The woman wasn't a fool," said Myra.

"Oh, you wouldn't have to be a fool, would you? You see, the Flavells feel responsible — well, they *are* responsible, aren't they? I mean — that is — " Eva realised what she had said and subsided into silence.

Vance came to her rescue. "I know what you mean. It must be terrible for Flavell, not only to lose his wife, but to feel he didn't take sufficient care in the first place."

"What else could he have done?" asked Carol indignantly. "He warned us to be careful. He said the ground was unstable."

Mr Sullivan shook his head sadly. "It should have been me that day."

Carol looked at Susan, saw her white face and guessed that, like herself, she was still in a state of mental shock. So were they all, of course. She leaned back in her chair, closed her eyes and let the comments float around her.

"I suppose we can all go home as soon as the interviews are over."

"Why did she go up there at all?"

"To see why Josephine fell."

"Perhaps she was going to sue the Council because of the ground being unsafe."

"It's the Council's property. They couldn't be sued."

"Yes, they could. Like when a burglar trips over your garden rake."

"She was worried about the reputation of the school. She didn't care personally what had happened to Josephine."

Susan plucked at Carol's arm. "Let's get out of here."

They walked outside and sat down on the stone cheetahs. It was a mild, gentle evening after the warm day, and the hills were still clear. They were silent. Susan was wondering why Rudy had to stay in the house instead of going to the lake with her. Was he just making an excuse? She was beginning to enjoy his company, and had thought he liked hers. Why did Carol distrust him so?

They had not been there long before Rudolph joined them. "How about that walk to the lake now, Susan? I'm free for a while."

"All right. Carol?"

"No, thank you." Carol sat looking after them for a few minutes, then got up and strolled listlessly round behind the house. John was sitting on the seat under the big oak at the side of the kitchen garden, looking over towards the hills. On an impulse she walked over and sat quietly down beside him.

He turned to her, and his face visibly lightened. "Carol! I'm sorry you had to — that this — "

"Oh, John." Their hands touched briefly. "I don't know what to say."

"You don't have to say anything. Not you." He stared at the hills again. "It was very generous of you to invite the students to stay on. Everyone appreciates it. But we're all leaving tomorrow."

He shook his head. "I'm not sure that's possible. There are — a few difficulties. There will be more interviews, further questioning."

"Why? I don't understand why they ask the things they do. And why do they tell us we don't have to answer if we don't want to?"

He turned to face her, and his expression was grim. "It's an obligatory warning in cases of homicide."

11

MISS PILLINGTON had breakfast with the students the next morning. She was less reserved now and chatted freely. There is nothing like a couple of sudden deaths for breaking the ice.

What Carol had learned from John was now common knowledge. Miss Pillington had been informed and had passed on the news. "The police say another person was present when Mrs Flavell fell off the bank," she told them. "There were marks of feet."

"You mean footprints?"

"No, not recognisable as such. Nothing clear enough to identify, but I think they've something else to go on. They say the matter is being treated as homicide. They even told the reporters that."

At first there was almost a sense

of relief. The unexplainable had been explained, a logical reason had been supplied for a puzzling event. The ground had not given way, the woman had not been idiotic enough to wander over the edge. It was really quite simple. She had been pushed. Then the full implication of it seeped through into their minds. Pushed! Someone had *pushed* her! Why? And who?

"Some madman from the village wandering about the grounds," said Eva. "An escaped lunatic. He climbed up there and went berserk."

"How could he get into the property?" demanded Vance. "He would hardly have just walked up the drive during the day. A stranger would be noticed at once. And the gates are locked each night. There's a high wall all along the road frontage."

"It could be climbed," argued Eva. "The Flavells don't put broken glass on top, like so many of the property owners round here."

"How do you know they don't?" asked Stein.

"Well — I'm sure they wouldn't. They're not like that. So he climbed over the wall and up the hill. The gate up by the quarry head was open so he walked through and pushed her."

"Rats!" snorted Myra. "She wouldn't be standing at the edge. Woman wasn't an idiot. So how did he get her into position? 'Kindly step forward two feet, madam — a little more to the left.' Rubbish!"

"He could have been up there before she came. She surprised him and he attacked her, and that's what made the marks on the ground."

"I don't believe it," said Myra. "And I bet the police don't. Else why do they want us to stay on here?"

Vance gasped. "Oh God, they don't suspect any of *us*?"

"Who else?"

"Who would want to kill her? Who hated her?"

"All of us," said Myra.

"Not to that degree," objected Vance. "She was an unpleasant woman, but she did us no harm. She was a jolly helpful teacher."

"Her husband might want to," said Myra.

"Oh no!" The cry came involuntarily from Carol. Stein looked at her searchingly. The beast, she thought. He knows I care.

Vance was saying, "He's certainly the only one to benefit. And she led him a dog's life, didn't she, Miss Pillington?"

"I had that impression. She used to shout at him. I had lunch with them, you know, and sometimes it was really most unpleasant. He didn't shout back, but he used to look daggers at her and say nothing."

"There you are then," said Myra. "He was bottling it up. He had good reason to kill her. None of *us* did."

Miss Pillington nodded. "He'll inherit the estate, and he won't have to close the school or sell the house. They used

193

to argue about that."

"Tell you what," said Myra. "Josephine fell. He thought what a jolly idea. My wife can do the same. That'll get rid of her nicely."

"Oh dear, I don't think he'd do that," said Eva. "The poor man looks so worried and strained. I'm sure he's very upset."

"So would anyone if he'd just killed his wife. Must be a shattering experience."

"I don't really think he did it," said Vance, and Carol shot him a grateful look. How horrible the whole thing was! John — who had a better motive? Suspicion was inevitable. Suspicion, questioning, possible arrest. She was annoyed that she felt so emotionally involved, and even more shocked that under her sympathy and her fears for him was dancing an irrepressible little thought that now he was free.

"Of course he didn't," said Eva. "It was a prowler."

"Could someone have done it by

accident?" suggested Susan.

Vance shook his head vigorously. "You don't accidentally throw someone over a cliff. And who'd go for an evening stroll with *her*?"

"The police certainly don't consider it an accident," said Miss Pillington. "They made that quite clear. And they've taken away a smock from the studio. I had to go up with them to get it."

"A smock? What the hell for?" Myra looked at Rudolph. "Mrs Flavell wasn't wearing a smock, was she?"

"No," he answered, and then added, "but Josephine Satterley was."

"Oh God," said Vance. "Don't you see? If Mrs Flavell was pushed, so perhaps was Josephine."

Stein nodded. There was a short silence as they stared at him. Then Eva said, "Why? No one would want to kill that poor girl."

"Her father's very wealthy," Miss Pillington reminded them.

Susan spoke up. "What's that to do

with anyone here? She didn't know any of us, she wasn't related — was she?" She looked round the group.

"If she was," said Rudolph, "the police will soon find out."

"A disappointed lover?" suggested Miss Pillington. "Full of bitterness and desire for revenge?"

"Then why kill Mrs Flavell too?" demanded Vance.

"She saw him kill Josephine?" suggested Carol.

"She'd have said so if she had," argued Vance. "No, there must be some relating factor. What did they have in common?"

"Why, nothing at all," said Eva, "and that just proves it was a madman on the loose, doesn't it?"

"Even homicidal maniacs have motives for their killings," said Stein. "They may seem odd motives to us, but they're compulsive. So even if a lunatic was responsible, the question remains — what was the common factor? They didn't both have red hair, or go duck-shooting or wear blue raincoats or disapprove of skateboards — "

Vance broke in. "There *was* one common factor. They were both on the short list for the Sanderson-Ebbings. It's conveniently shorter now."

There was a silence, then Carol asked, "Who else is on it?"

Mr Sullivan, who had hardly spoken during the discussion, now coughed gently and said, "I am. I assure you I don't win awards by eliminating the other candidates. Such a method had not occurred to me."

"Would *anyone*?" asked Susan. "That seems to be going a bit too far."

"It's a coveted award," said Vance, "worth a good deal of money. People have killed for much less." He looked at Myra, then Miss Pillington.

Miss Pillington responded. "I believe I'm on the list. You don't think — we're not — in danger?" A look of real alarm came into her face.

Myra said nothing, but her lips were curved in a slight acid smile.

Carol tried to keep her voice calm. "So John Flavell got rid of Josephine, then his wife, to better his own chances for the award? Is that what you think? And what about all the other candidates? Is he going to go round the county removing them one by one?"

"Actually there's only about three others," said Myra, "and they haven't much show. We all have a better chance with Josephine gone. She was the one most likely to get it. Why did the police want that smock? That's what I'd like to know."

Miss Pillington answered. "It's something to do with Miss Satterley's death, I think, because they asked me if that was the type she was wearing, was I sure, were all the studio smocks the same brand, and so on. I told them she was wearing one — she didn't bring her own — and I told them they were all ordered together from the same shop. They asked Mr Flavell to confirm that."

It became obvious during the morning that the police did indeed have suspicions about Josephine's death. There were further interviews. Where were they that morning before classes? What time did they get up? Where did they go first? Whom did they see? What time did they go down to breakfast? And then where, and when? Did they meet anyone on the way? Speak to anyone while there? The inspector seemed unreasonably annoyed at an answer that one 'didn't remember'. But how *could* one remember what one was doing several days ago? One day had at that time been much the same as another. There was nothing to make them remember minor events *before* the tragedy. They helped one another to sort it out, reminding of incidents, recalling conversations, mentioning small events which had led to others. 'You came with me to the front steps, remember? We were looking at the weather.' — 'You said you were going to the laundry.' — 'Did I? Then I must have. Oh, I remember now. Myra was coming back and I met her.' — 'I asked you for that book and you went upstairs to fetch it.' — 'Of course I did. I passed Eva coming down. That was just before breakfast.'

Gradually most of it fell into place. Times and whereabouts were established and noted down. But no one admitted to having been near the quarry head. And no one could prove positively that he had not.

They were asked to stay on. Oh, so politely, as if to grant a favour. But all knew they had no choice.

When you have lived and worked with a group of people for two weeks it is hard to regard them as other than normal, decent persons. You may suspect them of gossip, of envy, even of stealing your best sable-hair paint-brush, but that one of them should deliberately push another over a steep bank in order to kill is an idea hard to grasp. Murder is something which is carried out elsewhere — a newspaper filler, which you read about casually as you do the weather report or the situation in Iran. It doesn't occur among the ordinary kindly artists who pass you the marmalade with a smile. You don't expect roused passions and outbursts of violence in those whose chosen topic as they sip their coffee is the value of kinetic cubism or the influence of the Fauves.

The enthusiasm had gone out of painting. They went to the studio, they tried to occupy themselves with work, but no one's mind seemed able to concentrate on it, with the exception of Eva Tritt, who painted, chattered, and smiled. But then, as she told them, she was not worried. It was all very sad, but none of them was responsible. It was some poor demented soul from the village, and he would soon be caught and put under lock and key. "Or else the ground gave way," she told Carol. "The police see so much of murder that they suspect it when it's not there.

Mr Flavell fell, too, didn't he? No one pushed *him*."

"Yes," said Carol thoughtfully. "So he did." John had fallen, too. An idea began to shape in her mind and she watched for an opportunity to talk to him. He seldom came near the students now, but often wandered in the grounds, as if seeking solace from the wild flowers and the trees. She found him that afternoon down by the lake. He was sitting on the fallen log in front of the big cluster of rocks. It was one of his favourite spots. He was not painting, just sitting and gazing at the hills. She had a pang of sympathy as she saw his expression of despair. He looked exhausted, too. Had the police been grilling him? He *was* the obvious suspect for his wife's death, and they had a job to do.

He looked up and smiled wanly. "Share my log," he invited.

She sat beside him and for a few minutes they said nothing. It didn't seem necessary. Expression of sympathy was futile. She wished she didn't feel so deeply for him. Did any other woman feel the same? He was attractive, with that strong face, those twinkling eyes. She may not be the only one to be drawn by his appearance and his personality. She felt a twinge of jealousy. She must be careful not to stay too long with him herself, or gossip might arise. "How's your arm?" she began.

"Still weak. I have no strength in the fingers yet. But what does it matter now?"

"John, when you fell that day — when you came into the studio with your arm in a sling — you looked not just hurt, but puzzled, worried." She turned and looked straight into his eyes. "Tell me, John — did you simply fall, or were you — helped a little?"

He was silent for fully a minute before replying. Then he said slowly, "Carol, I honestly don't know. Does that sound unbelievable? It was all so quick. But I've been wondering. I was among the bushes at the far end, as you know. They're thick there, and I was pushing through them, and I *was* too near the edge. I knew that at the time. I had a new commission and wanted a fresh angle. I have a vague memory that just before I fell a bush had sprung back against my shoulders. I had at the time no reason to suspect anything else."

"But it could have been a push?"

"I don't know, I really don't. Would the impact of a human hand feel like that of a branch? I doubt it."

"But you wondered?"

"Not at the time. I found myself lying on the ledge, dazed and my arm hurting abominably. I was puzzled then only because I didn't see how I could have been so stupid as to step on the rain-sodden clay at the edge."

"If you were knocked out, you may not remember the last few moments before you fell."

"That's occurred to me, too. I

certainly didn't think then that I'd been pushed. But I'd had an idea that someone else was on the hill. That, too, was only a vague impression. I'd looked round twice and seen no one. It wasn't important. Students like to go up there. I may have heard the crack of a branch or a rustle in the bushes. I was intent on my own business, and it was of little concern to me who else was around. It wasn't until they said Miss Satterley might have been pushed over — "

"Did you suspect someone had killed Josephine?"

"No, not for a minute."

"Were there footprints of another person where she fell?"

"I doubt if anyone thought to look. There was one thing which I did wonder about. Why was she so near the edge in the first place? I was sure it wasn't suicide, but I didn't think of murder."

"Are the police giving you a bad time, John?"

"I've been closely questioned, but

that's understandable. I'm the obvious suspect for my wife's murder. I know that."

"Why would *anyone* want to kill her?"

He shrugged. "She made enemies. Annoyed people."

"You don't think it was to prevent her being chosen for that award?"

"That narrows it down too brutally. I can't think that. I can't think anyone capable of killing her deliberately, except some lunatic."

"That's what Miss Tritt says. A mentally deranged trespasser. It would need strength, wouldn't it? They'd have had to drag her to the edge."

"Or entice her. She wouldn't have strayed too close. She was careful."

"Have you told the police about your impression that someone else was present when you fell?"

"No, I can't be sure of it, and it might put suspicion onto someone who was in the area at the time for a perfectly innocent reason. More interviews, more questions. 'Where were you on the morning of — ' and so on. No, I don't want you all to have to go through that again."

"That's awfully decent of you, John, but in the meantime they may be suspecting you. Please tell them."

"I don't think they really suspect me. Inspector Lang strikes me as a pretty shrewd chap."

"Well, they can't connect you in any way with Josephine, can they?"

"I'd never met her until she came here. That can surely be proved. And however unwilling or ignorant my pupils are, I've never had the urge to push them into a quarry." He smiled. "You and Susan would have been over the first day if that was my practice."

"And no one would have blamed you." Carol got up. "John, I'm really a bit scared. Who's going to be next?"

He rose, too, but stared over the lake before he turned to her and answered. She guessed he had been wondering the same thing. "You mustn't be frightened, Carol. No one will go near the cliff edge now."

"There are other ways to kill. Oh, John, he's had one go at you and failed. Do be careful!"

"Carol!" He took her hand and held it tightly for a brief moment, then let it drop. "Look after yourself, too." He watched her as she climbed the slope towards the house, annoyed at his own feelings. She was only a student. What was it about her that made her safety so important? Nothing must happen to Carol, nothing. He'd paint her one day. It was a long time since he'd done a portrait. He'd do one of Carol and do it well. It would be accepted and hung. Because you did things well when your heart was in them.

12

CAROL walked slowly back to the house. It was a long way from the lake, and mostly uphill. She felt tired as well as depressed.

John had confirmed what she had suspected. However uncertain he pretended to be, he *knew* that someone had tried to kill him. He ought to tell the police. Three attempts at murder, and two of them successful. Was that the end of it? Was the killer's object achieved? Would he attack John again? Or someone else, someone already chosen as the next victim? The one thing that John, Josephine and Mrs Flavell had in common was their entry for the Sanderson-Ebbings award. John thought no one would kill because of that, but Carol was not so sure. Myra was on the list, and Myra gave the impression of ruthlessness and resolution. If Myra had a goal in sight she would let nothing stop in her way. Miss Pillington too was a candidate, and who knew what went on behind that sedate façade? She could be full of repressed ambitions and seething fury. They didn't know much about Miss Pillington. She had been so very reserved at first, and even now she was never addressed by her Christian name. And the others? Mr Sullivan? He wouldn't kill a fly! Or would he? Dr Crippen was said to have looked gentle and harmless. Then Rudolph Stein, whom she had mistrusted from the very first. He would make an efficient murderer — he had all the necessary qualifications. But no one was sure whether he had entered for the award. He was as secretive about that as about everything else. He could have entered late and not been on the published list.

Susan was in the common-room,

trying to read. "Come on outside, Sue."

"I'll be glad to. Where've you been? I get anxious when you're missing."

They walked outside and sat on the porch.

"I went to see John. Sue, he fell because someone pushed him."

"What? Why didn't he say so? Who did? How does he know?"

"He won't tell the police because he says he can't be absolutely sure. At the time he thought a branch had sprung back on him, and it wasn't until later that he began to wonder."

"You must *know* if you're pushed over a bank."

"You don't always remember what happened just before an accident. He says he found himself on the ledge, dazed. I think he was knocked unconscious on the way down. He'd roll and bounce down that slope."

"But that's three of them! Why, Carol, why? What's the connection?"

"They were all candidates for that

award. There are a few others in Sussex somewhere, but Myra says they haven't much chance. That leaves her, Mr Sullivan, Miss Pillington and — Rudolph, if he's in for it. So which of them did it?"

"It would be difficult, Carol. Not the actual pushing, but getting someone close enough to the edge in the first place, especially after Mr Flavell's fall. People aren't idiots where their safety's concerned."

"If they were dragged to the edge?"

"That would take strength. Myra could do it."

"So could Rudolph." The hurt look in Susan's eyes made Carol add, "But we're only guessing wildly." Her suspicion of Stein was growing all the time, but there was no point in trying to share it with Susan, who was so obviously attracted to the man that even her loyalty to Carol would not stop her from warning him, relaying others' suspicions. Then suppose he thought she was chattering too much?

A walk up the hill over to the head of the quarry — another accident?

"What's the matter, Carol? You look ghastly."

Carol pulled herself together. "I was imagining things. Sue, you won't ever go up to the quarry top, will you? No matter *who* asks you to?"

"I've no desire to."

"Promise?" Sue nodded. "Where's Rudolph?"

"He's in with the police again. I don't know why they're at him all the time. Finding the body, I suppose. Shall we go up to the studio?"

"I couldn't settle to anything there. It's all very well to be told to paint to keep your mind off other matters. It just doesn't work. That big room is like a ghost town. Mrs Flavell may not have been popular, but she used to make her presence felt."

"But Eva's there. She keeps on painting. I think I'll go. There's something I can work on. Rudy showed me how to carry on with it.

He says elongate the circles. It might make all the difference."

"I'm sure it would," said Carol absently. She sat for some time after Sue had left, but her thoughts seemed to twirl and interlock and tangle, like one of Sue's pictures. So there must be some meaning in them, she decided. I just fail to understand. My conception is limited. Too right it is. Come on, girl. Back to the common-room where you can at least talk about the weather to others just as confused as yourself.

As she was passing through the hall the door of the library opened and Stein came out. Confound the man. What did Sue see in him? In her momentary anger she walked straight up to him.

"Yes, Carol?" He looked at her enquiringly.

"I want you to leave Susan alone. I was the one who persuaded her to come here, so I feel responsible for her. I don't want her to have undesirable company."

"Undesirable?" A faint smile touched his lips.

"I have reason to believe," she bluffed, "that you are already known to the police."

His cold eyes seemed to pierce through her. He frowned.

"Well?" she demanded. "Do you deny it?"

"No. But I'll continue to enjoy Susan's company until she wishes otherwise. Excuse me." He sidestepped, passed her and strode outside.

Carol stood looking after him. She had made him angry, and that was dangerous. She *was* responsible. If anything happened to Sue it would be her fault. If only she could warn her, *make* her listen. She walked up to the studio. Eva was painting as composedly and cheerfully as usual. Sue was watching, and turned as Carol came in. "It was no good," she said. "I couldn't settle to work. I don't know how Eva does it."

"Nor I. That's a nice view of the

summer-house, Eva. How well you've done that creeper. And you've put a seat outside the door."

"Yes, it just seemed to need a rustic bench to set it off. Like Mr Flavell says, to make it look natural. I thought of a wishing-well, but I didn't know how to draw one, so the bench will have to do."

"The bench looks exactly right," Carol assured her. "Are you going to have anyone sitting on it?"

"Oh, I'm not *nearly* good enough for that. Perhaps a book lying open?"

"That's a good idea. Are you coming down now, Sue?"

"Right." They left Eva engrossed in her picture. "I don't know how she does it," said Sue. "It's not as though she was callous."

"No, I think she's really convinced that a trespasser is to blame for everything, and she isn't worried like the rest of us — not wondering all the time who it was, which of the students is a murderer. That's what bugs me most.

216

Sue, don't trust anyone, *please*."

"I shan't go up to the quarry top. I've told you so."

"I know you think I'm only prejudiced against Rudolph. But I've just spoken to him, and he couldn't deny that he has a police record."

Susan walked in silence for a while, her eyes on the ground. Then she burst out, "That doesn't mean much, and it doesn't affect what he's like now. It could have been shop-lifting when he was a kid — or — or getting into bad company once or being mixed up in a protest riot — or — " She stopped and faced Carol. "Well, anyway, he didn't murder anyone. He couldn't. And whatever it was he did in the past, I don't care. I'm not even going to ask him about it. He'll tell me when he's ready."

It was no use trying to convince her. Carol said nothing as they walked into the hall and over towards the common-room. Then she stopped and said, "Well, listen, Sue. There is a murderer loose. He's killed twice and he tried to kill John. I know John was pushed. He knows it, too. So be careful. Don't go wandering about the grounds alone."

"There's no reason for killing *us*," said Susan casually. "Are you coming up to change?"

"In a minute. You go ahead." She would see first if Vance was in the common-room. He saw a lot of Stein and must have formed an opinion about him. He may share her suspicions. She was standing there, hesitating, after Susan had left, when a shadow fell across her foot and made her start. Rudolph Stein was standing beside her, a curious expression on his hard face. She felt suddenly afraid. But he could do nothing here, within call of the common-room where others were sitting chatting, chatting about the murders *he* had committed. She tried to speak coolly.

"Have you done any painting today, Rudolph?"

He ignored this opening. His eyes

rested on her thoughtfully. She was intelligent, more intelligent than Susan. And she knew, or had guessed, too much. More than was good for her. He said, "So you believe that Mr Flavell was pushed over the quarry head?"

He stared intently at her and his eyes looked evil. Carol did not answer his question. Instead she asked contemptuously, "You were listening?" He stared at her still, and there was something strangely unnerving about his gaze. So this was how a snake mesmerises a bird, she thought. "I mean — you happened to overhear?"

"I did not 'happen to overhear'. I listened." The muscles of his face seemed to tighten a little and his stare became more intent. Then he said, "You are not to carry on with your speculations and theories and enquiries, do you understand?"

Carol's indignation rose. She was letting him scare her, stupidly, unreasonably. She wasn't a bird to freeze under the eye of this particular snake. What right had he to tell her what she should or should not do? "And why not?" she demanded.

"It could be dangerous to do so."

"Are you threatening me?"

"I'm warning you." Then he turned on his heel and abruptly left her. He hoped he'd said enough to frighten her off further interference. If not, he'd have to — take other measures. And that would be a pity.

Carol watched him go, and in spite of herself felt another little shiver of fear. His tone of voice had been that of one accustomed to being obeyed, and to eliminate any who questioned his orders. A gang leader, the head of a powerful organisation which would sweep away anyone in its way, as a housewife might sweep away an ant, and with as little compunction. She went into the common-room, but Vance was not there. She sat down and found to her annoyance that she was shaking. She was beginning to know real fear now. Stein had meant what he said. She had no doubt of that. Then she realised that one sensible course was open to her. She would report the whole matter to the police inspectors. If they knew he had threatened her, he would not dare harm her or Susan.

She would do it right now, before she went upstairs to change. The library door was open, so she knocked and walked in. "May I see you a minute, Inspector, or are you leaving now?"

Inspector Lang was tidying up papers on the table. "We don't work to regular hours, Miss Barton. Won't you sit down?"

So he knew all their names now? He should, he'd seen them enough. He was looking at her, politely, enquiringly. How did one accuse another person? She felt like a child telling tales at school. He may think she was merely trying to divert suspicion from herself. Well, there was something else she wanted the police to know, so she'd start with that.

"It's about Mr Flavell's fall. Before

you came, before Miss Satterley was killed — you know about it?"

He nodded. The other inspector was looking at her now.

"I'm quite sure it wasn't an accident. The ground did not give way."

"You're not the only one to reach that conclusion, Miss Barton."

"He knows it wasn't, too. I'm sure he knows he was pushed. He just doesn't want to say so in case it means more trouble and questioning for the rest of us. But he told me he had an idea someone was up there just before he fell and that he felt something on his back."

"I see." The inspector looked thoughtful. "He's said nothing to us about anyone else being present. That is most interesting. Thank you for letting me know, Miss Barton. We'll have another word with him."

"I hope he's not annoyed at me for telling you."

The inspector smiled. "I'm sure Mr Flavell will realise you did it in his best interests. It was very helpful of you to come and tell us."

Encouraged by his friendly manner, she went on, "There's one other thing. I've been threatened just now by another student — Mr Stein."

"He threatened you?" They were both staring at her.

"I don't trust him. He said — he — " She found her voice shaking.

"Take your time, Miss Barton." The inspector was fatherly, kind, and just a little patronising. "Now what's worrying you?"

As she spoke, it became easier. The words started to tumble out, her suspicions of Stein, his accent, her fears for Susan, and finally his words just now in the entrance hall.

"You felt he was threatening you?" The inspector smiled indulgently, as if humouring a child.

"He *was* threatening me. What shall I do?"

Inspector Lang's smile faded. He frowned, fiddled with his ball-point, and then said, "Heed his warning. Take no risks. Don't go near the cliff, and avoid voicing any theories of your own. But I don't think you're in any danger. You may be free to go home tomorrow. We're just waiting for a report from the forensic lab before we can make a definite announcement. In the meantime, don't worry."

"But he — he admitted — "

"Try not to worry, Miss Barton. And thank you for coming to tell us what you knew." He rose and opened the door for her, and she had no choice but to go out, dismissed, frustrated and annoyed. It had been a futile waste of time to tell him about Stein. He had summed her up as a neurotic young woman, and he simply didn't believe her.

13

THE next morning Carol was again in the library, this time by invitation. She was looking belligerently at the two inspectors. "They were different types and they sometimes disagreed over small matters, just as most couples do. But that was all."

"Do you know of any recent disagreement? Did you at any time hear voices raised, threats, quarrelling?" Voice, yes. Mrs Flavell had shouted at her husband within hearing of the students, and sometimes looked as if *she* could murder *him*. But voices, no. John spoke quietly and calmly to his wife. She felt justified in answering, "No."

"Thank you, Miss Barton. We need not keep you longer just now."

Carol rose wearily and walked to

the door. She turned there, wanting to burst out, '*He* didn't do it, I know he didn't.' But what good would that do? It would merely betray her interest in John. And — oh God, they might even consider her the Other Woman — a Motive. She didn't want to be a Motive. She went out and crossed over to the common-room.

Some of the others were there, and turned at her entrance. "Well?" said Vance sympathetically. "Where were you between two-fifteen and two-twenty-seven on the ninth, and what did you wear to breakfast on the Thursday, and why can't you remember whom you passed on the stairs on Saturday evening?"

Carol smiled weakly. "None of that this time. They kept asking me how the Flavells got on together. It was beastly. It isn't fair to ask us. We only saw them in the studio and at dinner."

"Can't blame them," said Myra. "They'll be asking us all. Hell, girl, it's a murder. Not like asking a school kid who stole the chalk."

"It must be terrible for poor Mr Flavell," said Eva. "Having his private life discussed as well as losing his wife."

Myra snorted. "Huh! Bet he's relieved to be rid of the old witch. She was a loathsome woman."

"Was that why someone killed her?" suggested Vance. "A community-minded citizen removing a public nuisance? Was Josephine disliked too?"

Myra shook her head. "None of us knew her well enough to dislike her."

"It should have been me killed, not her," said Mr Sullivan. "If I had gone up there that morning — "

"Oh, *do* stop saying that," broke in Myra. "There was no wandering trespasser. That's a convenient theory, but it doesn't make sense."

Eva protested. "Oh yes, Myra. Don't you think some poor mentally defective young man prowling about — "

"Why climb up there to indulge his

fancy for seeing people fall down cliffs? Don't be silly."

"There's nowhere else," Vance pointed out. "There are no cliffs in the village. If that was his hobby, he'd have to climb up the hill. But it would be a dreary wait, hiding in the bushes until someone came up and walked near the edge. Or did he lure each one? 'Come here, I've something exciting to show you.' or 'My poodle has just fallen over the bank. I need help. Quick!' But why? Just to see a person roll and plop? Like throwing stones into a pond? No, sorry, Eva, I can't agree with you. There's usually a sound practical reason for murder. Fear or gain. Who benefits by the death is always the first one to consider."

"Flavell benefits," said Myra. "Gets her money and is free of her nagging and doesn't have to sell the house and has a better show for the travel award."

Stop it, stop it, thought Carol. To change the subject, she said, "They took my fingerprints."

"Mine too," said Vance. "Routine, I suppose. They'll take everyone's."

"How tiresome," said Eva. "I do so hate the smell of ether. I think I'll go up to the studio again for a while." She trotted out of the room.

"Ether?" asked Susan.

"They clean your sweat off with ether first," Vance told her. "How did Eva know that?"

"Surprising old girl," said Myra. "Knows a lot of things. Widely read, too. Not as scatty as she seems. Well, they'll arrest Flavell soon and then we can all go home."

"Let's get out of here," whispered Carol to Susan.

They strolled outside, under the trees behind the house. "Don't worry about what they say," said Susan. "They've fastened on Mr Flavell because the alternative is one of them, and they're just unable to grasp that as a real possibility. I don't wonder. They're not like killers, any of them."

Carol would have excepted Stein, but she said no thing.

Susan was continuing, "And why *would* any of them kill her? Only Mr Flavell had a reason."

"He didn't do it, Sue, I know he didn't."

"You've really fallen for that guy, haven't you? Don't look so silly. It's not a crime. Unless you pushed his wife over the bank to make matters simpler. Perhaps some other woman did it for that reason — you know, a secret lover? Miss Pillington?" She saw Carol's face. "Oh, I'm sorry, Carol. I quite agree with you. He wouldn't be unfaithful to his wife, he's not the sort. And I like Miss Pillington. I like them all — all those who are left. The ones I didn't like much are the ones who were killed." She smiled dreamily, almost happily.

How selfish love renders a person, thought Carol. Susan was in love with Stein, and was going to be badly shocked when she was disillusioned.

In the meantime, the affairs of the others barely concerned her. Was she, Carol, in love with John? She could still think of the others and feel for them, feel so keenly that it hurt. If indifference to others was the basis for identifying love, she hadn't quite made it yet. And what were John's feelings for her? He was behaving with the strictest propriety. Just the occasional glance, phrase, touch. It is said that a woman always knows. But she didn't.

She glanced at Susan's serene face. The roles were reversed now. Susan was the stronger, relaxed and unafraid. Her friendship with Stein had given her confidence. She had said that the others could not grasp the fact that a killer was among them, but she behaved as if she didn't face the fact herself. Didn't she realise the very real danger? Of course, she had not seen Stein's face as she, Carol, had seen it — that cold, hard, menacing stare. What did John think of him? He must have summed him up.

That afternoon, when Stein had claimed Susan's company — and how could she prevent it? — she sought out John. To consult him about Stein, she told herself, and ignored the inner whisper which said, 'Don't kid yourself, woman. It's an excuse to see him again.' She found him in the grounds, and he strode up as if he had been waiting for her to come.

"Carol!" He looked at her bare arms. "Are you warm?"

He cares if I'm warm! His eyes are kind, concerned, more than that. "Yes, quite, thank you."

They began strolling naturally, as if they had met by design, through the trees and then down the slope towards the lake. There was no wind, the sun was out, and the valley presented an incongruous scene of peace and tranquillity. Carol felt the trees should rather have been wildly agitating their leaves in protest, and the wind shrieking a dirge.

"The police seem no further forward," said John.

"Does it hurt you to discuss it?" She looked at him anxiously.

He shook his head. "If I don't discuss it, I think about it. My wife and I had grown apart. We were never suitably matched. But the death of any person so near to one is like losing a part of oneself. Time heals, they say. That's nonsense. Time never heals, but the injury hurts less as the years go by. I know that. In a way it's a comfort to talk about it — with you, anyway. Carol, why do *you* think my wife and that girl were killed?"

"Could it have been jealousy? Your wife was a great artist."

"Yes, the best here, far better than me. I'm competent, but she had that extra something, that flair of genius. Who would kill for that?"

"Someone who didn't want her to have that award they talk of?"

"The Sanderson-Ebbings? That's possible, I suppose. Artists are like poets — easily roused and emotional. They can suffer great envy, imagined hurts, or a desire to balance up what they consider injustice."

"Are poets like that?"

"I'm speaking only generally. Most poets and most artists."

"*You're* not like that."

"I hope not. Nor is Miss Pillington."

"I'm not sure what she's like. She's such a nondescript sort of person. She seems to merge into the background. You forget she's there."

"She's level-headed, sensible and earnest — dully so at times. I doubt if she'd have the initiative to kill."

"Who does have?"

"You, Miss Hurst, Stein, Mackay. Have you seen Mackay, by the way? The inspector was looking for him."

"He's helping Mr Sullivan with his car. The handbrake's gone phut."

"What's wrong with it? Has it stretched or snapped?"

"I don't know, except that it won't work at all. When I left them they

234

were babbling about taking a 'clever spin'. What's clever about going for a spin without the hand-brake? It sounds stupid to me."

"A *clevis pin*. I didn't know Mackay was mechanically minded."

"He can do lots of things. John, we can eliminate old Mr Sullivan, can't we? He wouldn't kill anyone."

To her surprise John did not answer at once. He was frowning. Finally he said, "He would probably lack the strength more than the will."

"He's having a fit of conscience. He keeps saying it should have been him instead of Josephine who fell that morning, because he was going to go up there. He's going to tell the inspectors when he's next interviewed."

"I don't see how that will help them."

"No, but it's become an obsession with him. He assumes some mad trespasser was up there and didn't care which person he pushed over. That's Eva Tritt's theory, too."

"She's a nice, kind soul. It's good of her to go in to Hastings so often to pay accounts for the Ballins. I can't see her killing anyone."

"No. But what do you think of Mr Stein? I don't trust that man one bit."

"He's a well-known, talented sculptor, and his painting's good."

"Do you judge everyone by their artistic ability? I meant as a man."

"He seems all right. I hadn't really noticed. I concentrate on my students' work, not their personality. That is — normally." He looked at her and smiled.

"He's the only one who positively *looks* wicked. Of course, in books it's always the least likely who does the murder."

"In fiction, yes. In real life it's usually the most likely suspect, and in fact, Carol, in cold fact, *I* am the most likely person to have killed my wife. I'm the only one who benefits, that is, according to the world's standards.

I benefit financially, considerably so. And the world considers money the greatest asset, fallacy though that is. I don't really know why I haven't already been arrested. Of course, they're convinced Miss Satterley was also deliberately killed, and they must know I had no motive there. I'd never set eyes on the girl until she came here."

"Her fall could have been accidental, couldn't it?"

"Of course. The police are not familiar with the district. When they've studied the clay up there a little more they may decide it was just an unfortunate accident."

"But you don't really think so, do you?"

He turned to her. "Carol, I think we'd both be wise to say we do. If there's a killer loose — and there must be — it's dangerous to talk. Once having killed, a man finds killing easier. The provocation need not be so great. Over-confidence develops, and the need, or fancied need, for self-protection can persuade him to kill again and again. Carol, please don't voice any suspicions you may have. I couldn't bear any harm to come to you." He put his hand on her arm, then withdrew it quickly. "We'd better get back to the house. It's nearly tea-time."

The sensation of his touch on her bare arm lingered as they walked in silence back to the house.

14

"I'M going to tell them," said Inspector Lang. "Line 'em up and give 'em the facts. Cards on the table. It might upset the complacency of the killer and it could stimulate the memory of the others."

"The lab boys were quick, weren't they?" commented his assistant. "Can they match the smears with the paints of any one student?"

"It's no use asking them to try. It's cobalt, which Flavell says is the most widely used of all the colours. Even if they could detect differences between the tubes, the students borrow or pinch one another's materials, I imagine. Besides, there's paint all over the studio. On the easels, stools, chairs, walls — oils take days to dry. No, we can't pin-point it like that. Now, round them up, will you, Martin?

Don't bother with the Ballins — they're out of it. But all the rest in the common-room in half an hour's time."

★ ★ ★

Lang surveyed critically the group before him. They were sitting in a semi-circle, attentive, politely waiting. Each looked as a normal decent person would be expected to look in the circumstances — worried, concerned, slightly bewildered. But in his experience that was also the way a cold-blooded killer was wont to look. It was a pity. His job would be so much easier if they wore the record of their crimes on their face. A notch for each one, on the nose perhaps. He had read that the shape of the ears was an indication of the presence or otherwise of homicidal tendencies. Should he open with 'Kindly bare your ears, ladies and gentlemen'? But he had forgotten what the supposed formula was. They had not included it in his refresher course last year.

Miss Pillington sat neatly, her feet together. Everything about her was neat. She reminded Lang of a fastidious cat, paws together. She had only to curl her tail round to complete the picture. Flavell looked as if he hadn't slept. Miss Tritt had an eager expression, almost as if she were enjoying it. Old Mr Sullivan was working his hands together.

"You have been very patient," he began. "Thank you for your helpful co-operation. You may have been puzzled by the seemingly irrelevant questions put to you, so I've decided to tell you the progress which has been made in our investigations, and the reason we had to ask you to prolong your stay here."

He looked round the room for signs of reaction. Polite interest, enquiring eyes. Nothing more.

"You may be wondering why both deaths have been treated as homicide. There were, as you already know, strong indications that Mrs Flavell was not alone at the time of her death. But that was not all." Here he must watch them closely, watch for any signs of self-betrayal. His quick eyes went from one to another as he continued, "Approximately two yards from the edge of the bank, on the ground among the few bushes there, was a rather stout branch from an oak tree. It was roughly two foot four in length, and two inches in diameter at the thickest part."

Still no reaction, no sign of fear. He kept his eyes moving. "On the bark at one end of it were two faint smears of oil-based pigment, suggesting that the branch had recently been held in a hand. There were also fingerprints, not yet identified." No need to add that they never would be, that no print could show up on the rough surface of the bark. "That branch was sent to our forensic department for examination, and another interesting discovery was made." Watch them, watch each one. Their eyes particularly. It was the involuntary movement of the lids and the muscles round the eyes which sometimes gave them away. Mouths were more easily controlled. "Caught in the end of the branch was a small thread, hardly visible to the naked eye. That thread was found to be of fawn cotton."

Miss Tritt's mouth had fallen open. Mr Sullivan was biting his bottom lip. Flavell looked resigned, no longer caring. Pillington very attentive. Hurst aggressive. He went on, "Mrs Flavell was wearing a navy dress. This thread corresponds to those used in the weaving of the studio smock. Miss Satterley was wearing such a smock when she fell."

He paused for effect. No sign of alarm. He hadn't really expected it. "There is little doubt that Miss Satterley was propelled over the bank by the use of the stick I mentioned, and we have reason to believe that Mrs Flavell met her fate in the same manner." What reason? A personal conviction, mainly. But let them think there was factual evidence. "Well, that's the position. In view of what I've told you, if any of you have any information which you have not communicated to us, I beg you to come and see me. Think back over the days in question, try to remember details. Did you notice anything unusual before the tragedies? Any person acting strangely? Did you see anything out of the ordinary? Hear anything which puzzled you? However trivial you may consider it, please let us know."

He left the room.

Mr Sullivan was the first of the others to move. He got up stiffly. "I shall be driving into Little Dorley in about an hour's time to buy a new cable for my handbrake, which Mr Mackay has so kindly offered to repair. If any of you would like letters posted, or anything bought from the shops — "

"Thanks," said Myra. "I'll scribble a letter off." She left the room with him. John Flavell followed, and then Eva, announcing that she would do some more work in the studio.

"How does she do it?" asked Vance. "You'd think she would be the first one to have hysterics, and she's the calmest of us all." He stood up and looked at the others. "It's a funny thing, though — I feel I ought to be afraid that one of you is a killer. You know, wondering which, and what you're going to do next. And I can't. I just can't. I'd go walking up the quarry head with any of you."

"You're taller than any of us," remarked Stein drily. "I think we'd come off second best."

A remark in poor taste, thought Carol. Just what she'd expect of the man. She certainly wouldn't walk up there with *him*.

"So I've been thinking," went on Vance. "We've been assuming that there were just two possibilities — a stranger wandering into the grounds and going berserk, and one of the inmates of the house. But suppose it was an outsider with a purpose? Someone who knew the Flavells and Josephine and for some reason wanted to get rid of them all?"

"*What* reason?" asked Carol. "The Flavells had no connection with Josephine."

"Except for the art award. It all comes back to that, doesn't it?"

"Your theory's not practical," said Rudolph. "How did your outsider contact, and then lure up to the hilltop, each victim in turn? It would have been simpler to hunt them out and stick a knife in them."

"Not if you're a woman," said Susan. "We don't use knives."

Stein looked at her, and his face visibly softened. "What would you use then, Sue?"

"Nothing messy like a knife or a gun. Poison — barbiturates or something painless. Or pushing over a cliff, where you can turn away and not see the squash."

"Why use a stick?" asked Vance.

246

"Why not just go up and push?"

"That might be all right for you," Susan explained, "but a bit risky for a woman. Suppose your victim grabbed you? You might both go over. And you could get a better push with a stick. Even if someone was standing a few feet back from the edge you could run at them and the hard thrust in the back would make them stagger forward."

As the discussion continued, one thing impressed Carol. Apart from her own distrust of Stein, there seemed to be a surprising absence of suspicion among them. Knowing the facts the police had disclosed, they should have been eyeing one another with misgivings and fear. Had they failed to grasp the situation? They were none of them intellectually dull. They must be clinging in their hearts to the theory of a trespasser. She listened and contributed for fully another half-hour before she decided to go outside and look for John. As she left the room the arguments were continuing.

"Why would he leave paint on a stick, anyway? Wouldn't you wash your hands before you went out to murder someone?"

"How often do you wash your own? I just wipe mine on a turps rag until I shower before dinner."

"It was a faint smear, the inspector said. He might not have known there was any left on his hands. The laboratories pick up traces you can't see without a microscope."

John was under the trees at the back and came to meet her. "I was hoping to see you."

They sat down on the seat under the big oak. John said, "Carol, do take care, won't you? Do you lock your door at night?"

"I do now. But no one would have reason to attack Sue or me."

"What reason did he have to attack my wife, Miss Satterley or myself? Why *do* people murder? Fear or greed mainly."

"It couldn't be greed in Josephine's

case, could it? So was it fear?"

"Of what? Physical attack? That's unlikely. Blackmail? I can't see Miss Satterley in that role. What else comes under fear? Fear of exposure? Discovery of a guilty secret in one's past? A murder already committed, which only Miss Satterley knew of? No, of course not."

"Wait, John!" A sudden thought had struck Carol. "No other murder had been committed at the time of her death, but an *attempted* one had. She may have known who tried to kill *you*. She used to wander all over the grounds, and she could have been in the trees on the hill that day."

"I hadn't thought of that." He looked at her uneasily.

"Listen, John. Josephine wanted to tell Sue and me something the night before she died. She must have seen someone going up the hill after you. She didn't get round to telling us, though."

"Did she mention the name of anyone

she'd seen outside that morning? She may have done so before she decided not to tell you her suspicions."

Carol thought for a while. "I can't remember. I'll think about it. I'll try later to go over everything she said that night, but it was mostly casual chatter, and that's hard to remember."

"Yes, do that. The inspector seems to share your views about my fall. You spoke to him, did you?"

"Yes, I had to. You wouldn't do it yourself. You don't mind, do you? I told him you were uncertain. But I haven't told the others, except Sue, and I'd like to, in case they think — I mean they might — "

She found it difficult to finish the sentence, but he did it for her. "Might suspect me? Well, I suppose they do. They have every right to. Of my wife's death, that is. I don't know what advantage they imagine I could gain from killing Miss Satterley, though. Oh, don't look so alarmed, Carol. The police are competent, and the truth will come out in time."

"But you could be accused of killing Josephine because of that award. I know it's stupid, but that's what they might think, even the police."

"The award?" He laughed. "No one can suspect me for that reason."

"What do you mean?"

"I withdrew my application over a month ago."

Relief flooded over her like a warm, comforting blanket. "Why, John? Why did you withdraw?"

"I didn't really want to travel in those countries. The money would be useful. It tempted me, but I realised later that the greater temptation was simply vanity, the desire for prestige. And if I pulled out my wife would have one less rival."

"Do the police know you withdrew?"

"I imagine so. You've been worrying for nothing." He looked at her with a puzzled, anxious expression. "Carol, you didn't yourself think for a moment that I would — that I could possibly — "

"Of course not," she said quickly.

"Look at me, Carol." He put his hands on her shoulders, and she gazed into his eyes — deep grey eyes, unlike Stein's. "I swear to you by all that's holy that I did not kill my wife or Miss Satterley."

"I know you didn't. You couldn't kill anyone. But sometimes I have the impression — I rather suspect — that perhaps you know who did?"

He took his hands from her and looked away. There was silence for a few moments. Then he turned back. "I've said nothing to suggest that."

"I know you haven't. But you do suspect someone, don't you? You know who the killer is."

He paused again, and then nodded slowly. "I'm not going to name anyone, even to you. *Especially* not to you. But — yes, I think I know. And there's not an atom of proof."

"But John — "

"Carol, take care, do you hear? Don't go out alone in the grounds with anyone, *anyone*. And now you'd better go inside."

She nodded and gave him what she hoped was a cheerful smile as she turned to go. But his words had worried her more than he intended. Why *especially* not to her? Was it someone she knew well and trusted? Someone whom she would find it almost impossible to regard as a killer?

John stood watching her as she walked past the kitchen garden and round the side of the house, admiring her carriage, the shape of her head, the black curls setting off her fair skin and her large dark eyes. He wrenched his thoughts away. He must not let them stray along those lines. He was too old for her — too set in his ways — and probably under suspicion for murder as well.

15

MR SULLIVAN was not happy. The more he thought on the matter the more convinced he was that the Fates had spared him at someone else's expense. That someone else was, moreover, a young girl, whose adult life had barely begun. He was nearing the end of his. Elderly, they called him, but it simply meant old. So he could not approve the Fates' choice. They were a stupid, bungling trio, and if there *did* happen to be an after-life, and he was invited in by the management, he would forthwith seek them out and have a few sharp words to say.

A prowler had been on the loose, some half-wit with a frenzied lust to kill, an irresponsible maniac who had seen and seized an opportunity to throw two innocent fellow-beings down a quarry face. If he had gone up the hill that morning, he would have been the first victim. If both he and Miss Satterley had gone up, the trespasser might not have dared to attack at all. Then Mrs Flavell would not have gone to investigate later, and the second tragedy would not have occurred either. Even if he had gone alone that morning, he would not have so conveniently put himself in such a dangerous position at the edge of the bank — or he might have grappled with the killer. Well, perhaps his grappling days were over, but the fact remained, it was all very unfair.

Well, it was not he who had fallen, and now it was up to him to use to the full the years remaining to him. He knew it was assumed that at seventy-eight he had left ambition behind him, that he was quietly taking each day as it came and enjoying what it offered — sunshine, pleasant surroundings, and his own ability to reproduce on paper the aesthetic joy he felt. He'd made his name, he was well known and respected. But one never really retires. He had entered for the Sanderson-Ebbings award, and his chances were good. Two of the trustees of the fund were men nearing his own age, and had known him for years. Although they would not be guilty of favouring him through friendship, they had discussed the matter with him, accused him of laziness, and suggested that the stimulation of the award would force him to produce more paintings. The very fact that he had a shorter future than the other candidates was a point to consider. Yes, he had a very good chance of being chosen.

He was musing along these lines when he drove out of the Flavell estate and turned into the road. He had not invited anyone to come with him. He wanted to be alone for a while, to have no mention of murders, and to try to distract his mind by looking at the shops in the village. Besides the cable to pick up from the garage, he needed stamps, toothpaste, perhaps a few postcards of the district. He had asked permission of the police sergeant to leave the premises and it had been readily given, so the police too must consider an outsider responsible for the killings. He had no doubt himself. After working with a dozen people for two weeks, how could one fail to recognise a killer? And there was no killer in that house. The Ballins — quite respectable, and really too dull to murder anyone. Besides, from what he heard, they had an alibi on both occasions. The Flavells — Mrs Flavell was just possible to consider, but she'd been a victim. Miss Pillington — an earnest artist, good talent there. The students — no, certainly not him — no — and not her either.

The road began to descend gently, and he changed into second. The car window was open on his right; the breeze came in, refreshing, comforting, clearing his brain. He changed up to third again and drove along the straight stretch of road before the real descent began. Now the hill. It was a steep grade. He must change down. He gently pressed the brake-pedal in preparation. The car did not slow. He put his foot down harder — harder — pressing the pedal to the floorboards. The brake gave no response, and before he knew it he was over the brow of the hill and on the down slope. He disengaged the clutch, revved rapidly and pulled at the gear-lever. There was a sickening graunching — how he hated to hear a car in pain! But the second gear would not engage. He was back in third again. That garage hand had *warned* him to have the synchro cones attended to. What a fool he'd been! And letting the hand-brake get into that condition, too. He'd had the cable crimped once, and they'd told him it might not hold. But there'd never been any trouble with the foot-brake. He couldn't understand what was wrong.

The car was gathering speed. He tried again, pressing on the clutch-pedal, revving, and pulling urgently at the gear-lever. It was impossible to put the gears through. He mustn't panic. The car was in third, it was to some degree under control. It was only a matter of competent steering, negotiating the bends in the road until he crossed the bridge at the bottom of the slope and reached the uphill section the other side of the river. Then he remembered that the bridge had room for only one car at a time, and for about a hundred yards either side of it was a one-way road. He envisaged a headlong crash, with not only himself to suffer, but the occupants of the other car as well. Another young girl? Or a family with small children? He mustn't risk it. Anything but that! If he could only turn off beforehand, up a hillside? A deep ditch ran each side of the road, but there were farmhouses — there must be access to them — look for a culvert over the ditch. It flashed through his mind that he had insulted the Fates and they were taking revenge. He had criticised their choice of victim. All right, they were saying, you think it should have been you? Well, if that's the way you want it, anything to oblige. The car's speed was increasing alarmingly. He was pressed forward and beginning to sweat. Faster — faster — then he saw the open gate, a road over the ditch with a house beyond. This was it — now! He pulled desperately at the wheel. The car veered round, its tyres screaming in protest. The chassis knocked the gate-post, bounced off — along the drive. It was not metalled and the ruts made the car bump and jolt. Oh God, it was starting to *descend* to the house, straight towards it. But there were sheds on the hillside to his left. Turn up there — now — round — up, up — it was slowing, thank God, it was slowing — would it stop before it reached those buildings?

Then the car lurched against a barn and stopped. Mr Sullivan was thrown violently forward. The last sound in his consciousness was the indignant squawking of hens.

16

MR SULLIVAN'S absence at lunch caused no alarm. It was assumed he had preferred a snack at the pub in Little Dorley. It was not until mid-afternoon that Miss Pillington brought news of his accident. A local farmer had been roused from a leisurely inspection of his apple crop by the noise of his barn wall collapsing. Mr Sullivan had been taken by ambulance to the local hospital, suffering from concussion and head-cuts. It was fortunate that the farmer knew the Flavells, and that the presence of painting materials on the back seat suggested that the stranger was a student at the Summer School. He had rung John Flavell, who had at once gone round with Mr Ballins and towed back the car.

"Can we go to the hospital?" asked

Carol. "Will the police allow it?"

"There's no point," Miss Pillington told her. "Mr Flavell wanted to go himself, but when he rang the hospital they told him Mr Sullivan is still unconscious and may be for sometime."

"Oh, the poor old chap. How did it happen?"

"They don't know. They don't even know why he was calling at the farm. The farmer's never met him before. And they can't even understand *how* it happened. If he'd had a heart-attack and collapsed at the wheel, you'd think the car would go straight in the direction it was heading. But the barn was about twenty yards to the left of the track, and up a sharp rise. It's almost as if Mr Sullivan drove at it deliberately."

"They don't think he was trying to kill himself?" asked Vance.

"That's what Mr Flavell suggested. He says Mr Sullivan was showing severe signs of strain."

"We're all feeling strain," said Myra. "Man wasn't an idiot."

"He's fairly old," said Vance. "He could have had a lapse of memory and turned in there thinking he was on the road to the village."

Miss Pillington disagreed. "Mr Flavell says he can't possibly have mistaken that rough dirt-track for a public road. He's very upset. He's going to have the car repaired at his own expense."

"We're costing him quite a bit, aren't we?" said Susan. "Staying on, being fed, and paying no fees."

"Yes, he's a generous man," said Miss Pillington. "He told me there's no need for me to give any more tuition this session and my pay won't be affected. Of course, if I *can* be of help to any of you — Susan?"

Susan shook her head. "Thank you, Miss Pillington, but none of us seem able to settle to painting now, except Miss Tritt."

"Then I think I'll take my materials

outside now. There isn't much opportunity to paint when one is teaching." She left the room with a brisk step.

"She looks quite happy," remarked Susan. "It's almost as if she's *glad* of what's happened."

"I'll go and tell Eva about it," said Carol. "She's up in the studio."

Vance got up. "I'll come with you, Golliwog."

As they walked up the stairs, he said, "Perhaps Miss Pillington is just one of those people who can adjust quickly to tragic events. Do you think one can judge the character of the persons here by the way they're taking it?"

"And how *are* they taking it?"

He considered. "You, as I would expect — shocked, worried about others. Susan — very calmly."

"Yes, and that's surprising. She's usually the one worried about others. She's more composed than I would have expected."

"That's because she's in love," said Vance.

"With that awful man Stein? I hope it doesn't last."

Vance grinned. "What have you got against Rudy? He's a good sort. She could do a lot worse than Rudy."

"He's got a fake German accent. I don't trust him, and I don't like his beard."

"What's wrong with a beard? I had one last year. Rudy paints well and he plays billiards like a gentleman."

"How does a gentleman play billiards?"

"Like Rudolph Stein."

"He never mentions his family or his past."

"Why should he? Neither do I. That doesn't indicate a past which needs to be hidden. Those with a guilty history usually *do* talk about their past, a fictitious blameless past, carefully rehearsed."

"Huh! Well, what about the others? How do you think Myra's reacting?"

"I think she disguises her feelings. That bluff, hearty manner is often a

266

front for a sensitive nature."

"Eva's the one taking it best. Just going on with her work, cheerful and smiling. She's always the same."

Vance frowned. "Yes. Too much the same. She puzzles me. She's so much a type, almost a stage character. The kindly grandmother with a hobby. That would be an easy rôle to assume. She looks the part. But in my limited experience of kindly grandmothers, they're not so uncomplicated."

"You can't suspect *her*? She wouldn't kill anyone." But for a brief moment the idea of Eva as a killer did seem possible to Carol. John had looked so strange as he said 'Don't trust *anyone*'. He knew how friendly she and Susan were with Eva. That bland smile, like a fairy-tale witch luring little children to her oven. Oh no! "She wouldn't!" she repeated. "She's such a simple old dear, and genuinely kind."

"That's how she would aim to appear if she were putting it on. She's no simpleton. I think Rudy suspects her. He seems to watch her."

"*Him*! Bah!"

Vance laughed. "You'd be a menace on a jury, Golliwog. Prejudiced."

"He says those paint smears on the stick were cobalt blue. How does he know that unless he put them there?"

"If he *had* put them there, he would *not* know, because if he had known he wouldn't have left them."

"He might have remembered afterwards that he'd been using cobalt and that it could've been on his hands." They were at the studio door now. "Vance, before we go in, tell me, who do you really think did it?"

"Not you, Golliwog. You'd have started with Rudy. Not John or Susan or old Sullivan. By elimination, if I really *had* to fasten on someone, I think I'd say Eva Tritt."

But as soon as they walked in and saw Eva, Carol was convinced that his choice was ridiculous. Eva greeted them with a happy smile. "Have you come to paint? Oh, I do hope so. I get a little lonely up here, you know. No one else comes now. How nice to see you both."

"No one else can settle to painting, Eva. I don't know how you do it."

"Well, I don't want to waste time," explained Eva. "And I can't really help by *not* painting, can I? I mean, there's more to life than just being killed, don't you think? Now tell me, are those trees too dark?"

They told her of Mr Sullivan's accident, and she seemed genuinely sorry at the news. "Such a kind old gentleman, and such a *wonderful* painter." But she continued with her work as she expressed these views.

They stayed with Eva for a while, and then returned to the common-room. Everyone was restless, and the afternoon passed slowly. The inspectors had gone back to town, but strangers and uniformed constables were to be found where one would least expect them.

"There's such a lot of them," Carol

complained to Susan. "You just walk round a corner and some fellow's staring at you. We're all being watched, I suppose."

"No, Rudy says they assign a certain number of men to a case, and they just have to be on hand in case they're wanted."

Rudy says — Rudy says — Carol was tired of hearing what Rudy said. But she bit back the comment which sprang to her lips.

She could not sleep that night. Her mind kept turning over the possibilities. An outsider or — The list was limited. John thought he knew. Why had he said he wouldn't name the person 'especially to *you*'? That sounded as if it were someone she trusted, or associated with closely. So he couldn't have meant Stein. Would the killer try again? He'd failed once with John — oh, John. She would be going away from him soon. Would he suggest a meeting later? He had hinted at it. She couldn't bear never to see him again.

The grandfather clock in the hall below struck two. It was then she heard the sound from the corridor. A door had opened. Why? Each bedroom had a bathroom attached. An illicit love-affair, perhaps? She smiled to herself, pairing off unlikely couples. Vance and Miss Pillington? Myra and Stein? Stein! — Susan? Oh no, it hadn't reached those lengths. Susan wouldn't — would she? Susan was a 'square'. But if she were really in love. Carol sprang out of bed, went through the bathroom and listened at the door connecting it with Susan's room. There was no sound. She opened it softly and the moonlight through the gap in the curtains showed Susan's figure in the bed. Greatly relieved, she returned to her own room. She felt wide awake now. She went over to the window and looked out. The moon was bright and the fields visible in the distance. The intervening trees looked ghostly, eerie, their shadows dark in contrast. It was all rather beautiful.

Then she saw a figure cross the kitchen garden and duck behind a clump of trees. It looked very much like Rudolph Stein. Looking for another victim? No one believed her when she said he was not to be trusted. Not Susan or Vance or even John. She was suddenly angry. And anger drives out fear. She put on her dressing-gown and opened the door. All was quiet. The corridor and stairs were dimly lit by a low-watt bulb which burned at night. She went softly down the stairs, and a cool draught of air met her. The french windows of the games-room must be open. She walked through the room and outside. The air was fresh, chilly. Everything looked different in the moonlight. It would make a wonderful painting. Of course! Someone was simply studying moonlight effects for a new canvas. Even Stein could do that. Night scenes must be terribly difficult to do. It wouldn't be Stein, it would be Eva, that irrepressible enthusiast. But why wait until two o'clock in the morning? The moon had been shining before they went to bed. No, it was no one taking notes for painting. She crossed to the clump of trees where she had seen the figure disappear. The silence was heavy, complete. Then a slight rustle behind her made her swing round in fright, her heart pounding. A small animal scuttled across the track. A stoat. But the experience had made her realise that she was not as brave as she had thought. The shadows were so very dark. She should at least have brought a torch. Anyone could be lurking there. She was a fool to have come. It was cold, too. She would go straight back to the house and into bed.

She pulled her dressing-gown tightly around her, and suddenly had a chilling conviction that she was not alone. She was standing in a shadow. If she moved out of it she would be seen. It was just possible that whoever was prowling around the trees did not know she was there. But would not he, too, sense the presence of another? Why had she been such an idiot as to come outside? Would she be dragged to the quarry top and thrown over? Ridiculous. Her fighting spirit returned. He'd have to gag her first, or knock her out. She would prove a struggling weight, not like Josephine. By the time he'd got *her* halfway up the hill he'd be sorry. She'd bite his hands, she'd kick, she'd — anyway, he wouldn't get as far as that. She'd scream if he so much as came within a few yards.

Then suddenly a figure was coming towards her. She didn't scream. She couldn't. Her voice froze with fear in her throat. She stood motionless, unable to move. The figure stepped out into the moonlight, and she saw it was Rudolph Stein.

"G-go away." The words came out faintly, as a hoarse croak.

"What the hell are you doing here?" said Stein. "Get back to the house at once."

"I — it's — " She stood straight, pulling her gown round her, and then managed to say, "If you come any closer I'll scream."

He stopped where he was. "Go back inside," he ordered. "At once. Hurry up. Go back to your room and lock the door."

She backed away from him, slowly, step by step.

"*Now*," he said. "I don't know how you came out, but the games-room window is open. Go back that way. And don't be such a fool as to come outside again during the night. Go ON!"

She turned then and ran. Thank God, the window was still open. She was panting, her heart beating rapidly, as she ran up the stairs and into her room.

17

FRIDAY dawned overcast and chilly. "At least it gives us a talking-point," said Susan. "We can tell one another what a rotten summer it's been. It's becoming difficult to talk about the murders, isn't it?"

"That's because it's finally penetrating our thick skulls that one of us was responsible for them."

"And *you* think it was poor Rudy. I know you do."

"I haven't said that. But your 'poor Rudy' was roaming outside at two o'clock this morning."

Susan stared. "How do you know?"

"I saw him from my window, and — " Carol stopped. Susan was so one-eyed about Stein that she might resent her following him out.

Susan had already turned to face

her, her cheeks pink with indignation. "How do you know it was Rudy? And if it was, why shouldn't it be? I bet if it *was* Rudy, and it probably wasn't, then he had a jolly good reason and you've no right — "

"All right, all right," Carol broke in. "I was just mentioning the fact. I wonder how Mr Sullivan is this morning?"

"I haven't heard." Susan sounded sulky, quite unlike her usual good-humoured self. It was useless trying to convince her that her precious Rudy was up to no good.

"I think I'll go and ask John if he's heard anything more."

"That's as good an excuse as any," remarked Susan.

Carol did not reply. The comment was only too true. But she did honestly want to know how the old man was, as well as to be with John. She found him in the common-room, talking to Vance. Vance grinned and deliberately left them together, going across the room to talk to Myra Hurst. So her interest in John had not passed unnoticed? Well, what did it matter? "John, how is Mr Sullivan? Have you heard?"

"Yes, I was just telling Mackay. He's still unconscious, but they don't seem too worried. He's not in the Intensive Care any more."

"Poor old chap. John, Stein was outside last night." She told him what had happened.

"What came over you to go outside at that hour? I *told* you — "

"I was angry, and it wasn't until I was actually out there in the moonlight among the trees that I got scared. Anyway, he didn't hurt me. He just ordered me back to bed."

"And very sound advice. Please don't do anything so rash again, Carol. I have to go and talk to Ballins now, so I'll see you later. Now, you remember what I've told you, and take care."

"I will, don't worry." She watched him go out of the room, and then

278

realised that Vance was standing at her elbow.

"Myra's in a bad mood," he said. "She tried to pick an argument with me because Stein's not here to fight with her."

"Arguing with him is her form of relaxation, I think. Everyone's edgy now. Vance, Rudolph Stein was outside last night, roaming round in the early hours of the morning."

"Oh? How do you know that?"

She told him. "And if that doesn't prove he's a fishy character — "

"You were very brave to go out after him, Golliwog."

"I wasn't brave at all once I was out there. I was scared stiff. I couldn't even scream when he appeared. But what was he doing outside at that hour? He was fully dressed. Doesn't that show he's a criminal? I knew he was. He as good as admitted to me once that he's known to the police. I can't understand why they haven't arrested him by now."

"He's OK," said Vance casually. "Come up to the studio with me? I promised Eva to go. She wants help with those trees in her painting."

As they passed through the hall, they saw Stein just going into the library with Inspector Lang. So the inspectors were back again! They hadn't stayed away for long. And they were on to Stein now, Carol thought in satisfaction. He wouldn't get away with it. And as soon as she'd seen Eva she'd go and tell the inspector about last night. He'd listen *now*.

Eva was not in the studio. "She could be painting outside," said Vance.

"In this weather? Oh, Vance, you don't think — "

"Of course not. She'll be all right. Don't worry, we'll find her."

They returned to the common-room, and Susan hurried up to meet them. She looked very distressed. "Have you heard? They've arrested Eva!"

"*Eva*? Oh, no! She didn't — they couldn't. Who told you?"

"Miss Pillington. I can't believe it, Carol. Not Eva!"

"Of course not. Miss Pillington must have got it wrong."

"No. She says she was in the studio when the inspector and a constable came in and got Eva. They gave her an official warning, she thinks, but she couldn't hear it all because she was up by the dais. Then Eva said, '*Me*? You're arresting *me*?' and went off with them in a sort of daze."

"They're crazy. Eva wouldn't kill anyone. Why pick on her?"

"They wouldn't arrest her unless they were sure of their ground," said Vance. "They can't afford a mistake."

"They've taken her away? She's gone?"

"No, not yet. She's packing, Miss Pillington says."

"Oh, poor Eva. I can't believe she's guilty, I just can't. Sue, let's go and see her. I'd like to hear what *she* has to say about it. If she says she didn't do it, she didn't."

"The police don't make arrests lightly," said Vance. "But of course she'll deny it. I'd better come with you."

Carol bridled. "You're afraid she'll go mad and attack us, I suppose? No, thank you. Come on, Sue."

They went up to Eva's bedroom. The door was ajar and a uniformed constable stood outside. "May we go in, please?"

"Sorry, miss. No one's allowed in. Sergeant's orders."

There were sounds inside the room of drawers being opened and closed. "Just to say good-bye?" pleaded Carol. She tried to peer round the door, and he stepped in front of her. "Sorry, miss. I'd like to oblige, but it's more than my job's worth. Serge is in there with her."

"Oh." If the sergeant was in the room it was no use trying to persuade the constable. They walked slowly back downstairs. "I'm going to go and ask Inspector Lang," said Carol. "I want to see her. I just want to hear her say she didn't do it. Then I'll *know* she didn't."

Inspector Lang was just going into the common-room. Carol put her request.

"No reason at all why you shouldn't say good-bye," he answered readily. "If you care to wait in the hall you can speak to her as she goes out."

Only a few minutes later Eva and the sergeant came downstairs. The constable followed, carrying a suitcase and a travelling-bag with canvasses poking out of it. It was the sight of these which touched Carol most. Eva had loved her painting.

"Why, hullo, girls!" Eva beamed at them. "You know they're taking me away?"

"Yes, but we both know you didn't do it."

"Oh, but I'm afraid I did," said Eva cheerfully. "Like they say in books, 'a fair cop', eh, sergeant? I had it coming to me. I shouldn't have expected to get away with it. Never mind, I'll plead guilty and they may take that into account. It saves the police such a lot of trouble when you plead guilty, you know. They like to show their gratitude."

Carol and Susan were silent. The shock of the admission had taken their power of speech away.

Eva went on, "I'd love to see you when I'm inside. That is, if you could spare the time. I don't want to ask too much, but I *have* so enjoyed your company — and if you — of course, it's not nice being seen visiting a prison — might give you a bad name — I wouldn't want — " Her voice was faltering more and more and her face dropping as she looked from one to the other and saw the shocked disgust. "It doesn't matter. I'm sorry, I shouldn't have asked."

How is one expected to react to a murderer's invitation to pay a social call? Carol felt repulsed and a little sick. "We live in London," she said weakly.

"We'll be back at work and rather busy," added Susan.

Eva's eyes suddenly filled with tears, and Carol felt a momentary pang of sympathy. After all, the poor woman must be mentally unstable, and not responsible for her actions, and she'd have a long sentence to pay for them. Then she thought of Josephine, and the sickness welled up in her again. The killer of Josephine! And would-be killer of John! She turned away.

It was only Susan who watched as Eva was led out of the door. It was only Susan to whom Eva could give a wan wave of farewell as she climbed into the police car.

18

"**A**T least we don't have to be afraid any more," said Carol. "Or suspect everyone we talk to. That was the worst part."

"And *you* suspected Rudy!"

"I'm sorry, Sue. It was that phoney accent. Why did he put it on?"

"I never asked him. He doesn't have it when he talks to me."

"Oh, Susan." Carol looked with exasperation at her friend. So simple and trusting. Of course she hadn't asked him. She thought the best of everyone, and the shock of Eva's guilt must for that very reason have hurt her more than anyone else. Carol could still see the hurt look on Eva's face when she knew they didn't want to visit her. But what else could she expect? The woman was a monster. That benevolent attitude, that apparent

286

kindness, was all put on. This explained some inconsistencies in her behaviour, the occasional lapse from the rôle she had chosen, of simple, harmless, middle-aged spinster.

"We can leave now," Carol said. "We can pack up and go."

"Y-yes. But shall we have lunch here first? I want to see Rudy and I suppose you want to see John."

Carol admitted, "Yes, I do. We'll say good-bye to them both after lunch." She secretly hoped it would be to make arrangements to meet again. She was confident John would want to. "I know what we can do now. We can go up to the quarry top and look at the sea, without feeling that anyone might be going to poke us over. It won't be out of bounds any longer."

"Right. I'll show you how to analyse a seascape into abstract design. It's not as nutty as we used to think, Carol. Rudy says — " She stopped as she caught sight of Carol's face. "Sorry. I wish you liked Rudy better."

Carol said nothing. At least Stein wasn't the killer. Let Susan keep as much of her simple trust as she now had left. She wished she had more of it herself. She had suspected nearly everyone in turn. How beastly one was, really, always ready to think the worst of others, to imagine they would do what you wouldn't do yourself. Or would one, if pushed to extremes? She still didn't trust Stein, even now that she knew he was no murderer. If he tried to hurt Susan, to what extent would her desire for revenge carry her? As they walked up to the top of the hill, she was idly wondering whether she could ever feel a strong enough urge to push Rudolph Stein over a cliff. Then they looked up and saw him.

"Rudy!" said Susan, with a delighted smile.

"*You*!" said Carol coldly.

Stein looked as surprised as they were. "What are you two doing? You were told not to come up here."

"That was *before*," said Susan. "It's all right now, isn't it?"

"Of course not. It's still out of bounds. And before *what*?"

Carol felt a surge of anger. Perhaps she *would* push him over. "Then what are you doing here yourself?" she asked sharply. "And shouldn't it be 'bounts'? You're forgetting your accent."

He grinned, without appearing to take offence. "The need for it has gone. And we're all out of bounts. Come on, back to quarters. I'll take you both on at table tennis. Vance tells me you're hot stuff at it, Carol."

She opened her mouth to snub him with a pithy, flattening retort, but the words didn't come. Pithy retorts have a habit of arriving too late for use. He was chatting on, his whole manner relaxed, more friendly than she had ever seen him before. That's the way he had always been with Susan, she supposed. Everyone would be more relaxed now. She suddenly felt at ease herself, as if tight elastic bands round her head had been cut through and the pressure relieved.

Susan was speaking. "It's awful, though, isn't it, Rudy? Eva Tritt of all people!"

Rudolph laughed. "Oh well, as she said, she asked for it."

"That's one way of putting it," said Carol, glaring at him. "I suppose pushing a few people over a precipice *could* be called asking for trouble."

"What *are* you talking about?" Stein stopped still and turned to her. "Oh Lord, you didn't think — " He looked from one to the other and his face grew serious.

"They've arrested Eva," said Susan. "Didn't you know?"

"Of course I knew. I was responsible for it. But — " he paused, and then said — "I rather think you have the wrong idea. Eva Tritt has been arrested for being in possession of, and for passing, counterfeit five-pound notes."

★ ★ ★

The fear had returned. They were in the common-room now, Myra, Vance, Carol, Rudolph and Susan. The last two were sitting close together, and Carol envied Susan. If John were sitting by her she too would feel protected.

"So you're a dick?" Myra was saying, and gave her loud, horsy laugh.

"On vacation," said Stein mildly.

"And you came here to nab the Tritt?"

"Certainly not. I came here to paint."

"Why did she come here to pass her notes?"

"She didn't. *She* came to paint. And because she'd been several times before and was well known to the Flavells, she took the opportunity to pass notes by driving in to Little Dorley and to Hastings to settle accounts for them. Can't you just imagine her with the Flavells or the Ballins? 'I mislaid the cheque you gave me, and I happened to have enough cash on me — here's the receipt — and now I've found your cheque, so perhaps if you made it payable to me?' or 'I'll pay them and you can reimburse me later.' Or with the shopkeepers, 'Perhaps you'd rather have cash? I have enough here, and if you endorse the cheque — ' What busy shopkeeper wouldn't jump at the offer? Yes, there were various ways in which she could gradually exchange her counterfeit for good notes. She was getting rid of it so successfully that she contacted her associates and suggested they bring her another batch. The outgoings here are quite substantial, and both the Flavells and the Ballins trusted her completely. They had no reason to do otherwise, because the accounts were paid and the receipts produced. They considered it very kind of her to go to so much trouble."

"We all did," said Carol. "So that's how she knew there was no broken glass on top of the wall? She must have taken steps to find out first. But if you knew what she was doing — "

"I didn't for a while. But I recognised

her. I'd seen her in the dock, though I couldn't remember the circumstances. I was afraid she might recognise me. If she was going straight it would be embarrassing for her. If she wasn't — well, I *am* a policeman. I have a German name, and Susan told me you considered me a German spy, Carol."

"You rotter, Sue!"

"I didn't tell him all the horrible things you said about him."

"So why not encourage the image?" went on Rudolph. "Like will to like, and if Miss Tritt was engaged in some criminal activity she might give herself away to someone she imagined was a foreigner fleeing the law of his country. Then I finally remembered what she'd been charged with, and I asked her one day to change a twenty-pound note for me. She said she had no change, yet I'd seen her with a bundle of notes in her hand. She was too shrewd to risk handing over counterfeit where she was known. So I guessed she was up to her old tricks. Criminals tend to specialise

293

and stick to the same sort of crime."

"So you put on a foreign accent?"

"At times. If my accent came and went I was more likely to be regarded by her as a fellow crook."

"Sneaky," said Carol. "How did you catch her?"

"I kept watching her. By sheer luck one day I heard her on the phone saying, 'It had better be at night, because the fuzz are crawling round all day. You'll see an old summer-house . . . ' That was all I heard, because she saw me and I had to walk on. No date, no time. But it was to be at night. And only evil fears the light."

"That's quite poetic," said Susan. "You've been talking to Vance."

"I shouldn't have said 'evil'. It's too strong a word. Eva Tritt is by no means evil, just dishonest. I watched her more closely, listening at night. I didn't have much sleep. Then on Thursday night I heard her door open."

"Oh, that was when — "

"Yes, Carol. You nearly ruined it. I'm sorry I had, to be so curt. I had to get rid of you and be on my way."

"And you caught her?"

"She met a particular gentleman well known to us. I let him go. We can lay hands on him whenever we want. He's being tagged and we hope he'll lead us to bigger game. I kept in the shadow until he left and Eva Tritt was on her way back with a bagful of notes."

"Did Inspector Lang know you were watching her? Is that why you were always such a long time being interviewed?"

"Lang and I are old friends. I'm in a different branch, though."

Myra said, "So Josephine and Mrs Flavell got on to her, and she had to dispose of them?"

"Good Lord, no. Eva Tritt's no killer, and on the morning Josephine was killed I happened to be watching her. I can give her an alibi myself."

"I knew she wouldn't kill," said

Susan. "Poor Eva. What'll happen to her?"

"A term inside this time, I should say. It's a second offence."

"Well, I still like her."

"As a matter of fact, so do I," said Rudolph. "Don't worry about her. She's a cheerful soul. They may let her paint in prison."

"And we *will* go and see her, won't we, Carol?"

"Of course we will. She was awfully nice to us. Only, now — " she shivered — "we're back where we were, aren't we? There's still a murderer loose."

"Unfortunately, yes," said Stein.

"John Flavell was pushed too, did you know?"

"Lang told me about that."

"I thought as much," said Myra. "Flavell's no fool. He knows the ground up there. He wouldn't be stupid enough to tread on an undermined portion, and even if he did he was at the end where the scrub is. He could have grabbed at a bush if he felt his feet going. But not if he was unexpectedly shoved in the middle of the back. So which of us did it, eh?"

They all looked at her, shocked by the question. She went on, "No use beating about the bush. Face facts. The Ballins are out of it. Tritt's out, Flavell's out. That leaves the Pillington, Sullivan and the five of us."

"It wasn't *any* of us," said Susan. "It was an outsider, wasn't it, Rudy?" Her question had an appeal in it.

He did not answer her. Instead he got up and said, "I'll go and have a word with Lang. He may have news of Mr Sullivan."

When he had left, Carol turned to Vance. "Did you know who he was?"

"Only two days ago. He told me then."

"And you didn't tell us!"

"I gathered it was confidential. You and Susan were so friendly with Eva that he couldn't trust you to keep it quiet."

"But he trusted *you*."

297

"Some people do."

Susan turned to Myra. "You shouldn't have said 'the five of us'. That included him."

"So what? Being in the police force doesn't give him an alibi. All right, girl, don't look so indignant. I'm not saying he did it. As a matter of fact, I'd go along with your idea of a prowler. Some half-wit. Saw Flavell at the top of the quarry — gave him a shove. Came back one day — saw Josephine standing there, picked up a branch lying around, pushed *her* — getting the feel of it now — came back — branch still there, saw Mrs Flavell — " She stopped, then shook her head. "I say, this doesn't make sense, does it? Each one lined up ready and waiting when he happened to stroll up."

"Then who *was* it?"

The discussion began again. Carol closed her eyes. They'd been through it so often before. It got them nowhere. John had asked her to go over again in her mind everything Josephine had said the night she came to see her and Susan. She'd tried and tried. But her brain was clearer now. The brief respite, the all too short period of relaxation, had refreshed her and she may remember better. She let the voices of the others fade into the background as she leaned back in her chair and went over the scene again. Josephine coming in — could she speak to them — something she didn't understand. They'd given her tea — asked about her painting — suggested a typing course — none of that was any help — spoke of the way she walked about the grounds, moping, dodging people she saw — people she saw — the morning of John's fall. She *had* seen — oh God, no! It couldn't be!

"Wake up, Carol!"

She opened her eyes. They were all looking at her.

"This is no time to go to sleep," said Susan.

She felt weak and shaky. She mustn't

let them see. It was only a mad idea. It didn't prove anything, either. And the big question remained — *why*? What could the motive be? It didn't make sense.

"Weren't you listening?" said Susan. "Vance thinks Josephine may have pushed Mr Flavell in a fit of temper, because he was trying to teach her and she hadn't wanted to come on the course, and then she got awfully remorseful and committed suicide. She was worried about *something* that night she came to us. We didn't think of that."

Carol forced herself to look at Vance. "And Mrs Flavell?" she asked in a weak voice.

"Accident," he said. "Pure accident. She was examining the ground to see why Josephine fell and she simply tumbled over."

"Won't wash," said Myra. "Woman wasn't a halfwit. And what about the stick with the paint on it?"

Carol hardly heard. No motive, she

was thinking. No motive at all. So it just *can't* be —

"Oh, we're getting nowhere," said Susan. "Neither are the police, it seems. I don't think they'll ever solve it."

"I wouldn't say that," said Vance. "They have got to get all their facts together, collect little bits of information and evidence."

"Then fit them together, you mean? Like a jigsaw?"

"Not exactly like a jigsaw. In a jigsaw you use *all* the pieces. The police must pick up a lot of irrelevant information — like Eva's business, for instance. No, I think it would be more like painting a picture. You look at the landscape before you, all the detail, and without letting yourself be distracted by parts of it you pick out the features pertinent to your theme, rearrange some, ignore some, relate some to others, until you have your integral, unified picture, the scene you're looking for."

"I get you," said Myra. "Hey, Carol, what's up?"

Carol was sitting bolt upright, eyes wide, her mouth half open, star[ing] at the far corner of the room. She h[ad] a dazed, half-frightened expression.

Susan exclaimed, "Carol, wh[at] bitten you?"

Carol turned to her slowly. Her f[ace] was drained of colour. "That's it," [she] murmured. "That's why. Painting – [the] picture." She got shakily to her fee[t.]

"What's the matter?" Susan r[ose] too. "Carol! Are you ill?"

"No, no. I — excuse me, I m[ust] think." She walked to the do[or,] unsteady on her legs. "No, do[n't] come, Sue. *Please*. I want to th[ink] something out. I'm quite all right."

"Can't I — "

"No, please, Sue." She turned at [the] door, white, visibly trembling. "I'm j[ust] going outside for a while. If I w[alk] about and think — "

The door closed behind her, [and] Susan stood, hesitating. Vance pu[t a] hand on her arm. "Let her alo[ne,] Susan. She asked to be alone."

302

"But what's got into her? She looked terrible."

"Reaction." Myra shrugged the matter off, and Susan felt annoyed at her attitude. But Vance agreed. "Myra's right, Susan. It's been an awful strain on all of us, and it takes people different ways. Carol's been putting a good face on it, and now she's having a fit of depression. She may simply feel like crying her eyes out under a tree, and I guess she doesn't want an audience for that, not even you."

"I suppose you're right," said Susan doubtfully. But she was still staring, puzzled, at the door.

19

CAROL went outside. It was dull and cold, but the wind had dropped. She pressed her hands to her temples. She must think — *think*. Her first impulse was to find John, who would probably be outside, and painting. She knew his favourite spots and he should not be too hard to locate. He was not on the seat under the oak at the back of the house. She passed through the trees behind and saw him in the distance, down by the lake. He was sitting on the fallen log by the big rock in front of the grove of beeches.

As she walked down the hillside towards him she tried to put some order into the thoughts which were tumbling so confusedly in her mind. She was reminded of those puzzles with little metal balls, all rattling round haphazardly until one can manoeuvre each into its slot. Before she talked to John or anyone she would like to get her ideas into their proper slots, too. One by one they were dropping into place. She walked slowly.

By the time she reached him her head was clearer and she felt calmer in herself. A sketch-block was on his knees and paints by his side. "Carol." He looked up at her with a warm smile. "Please excuse me from getting up. It would involve the displacement of a pad, several brushes and a dinner-plate."

"A dinner-plate?"

"Which I'm using as a palette. I prefer a white surface. I have another commission for a lake scene, and working with you has revived my interest in water-colour. It's a lovely medium. I'm doing a colour sketch to work on later."

She looked at his pad. "Is that really only a sketch? It's beautiful, just beautiful." It was one of those deceptively simple paintings which have an instant impact, and which only water-colour and superb talent can produce. Ethereal, transparent, magical. One of the best she had ever seen. She knew she had better appreciation now and was capable of judging it to be so. Had she never come on the course she would still have liked it, but would not have understood how much skill lay behind its production.

He had rearranged the landscape a little, but the essence of it was the scene before them — the hills, the trees, the dinghy, and a portion of the lake. "Those greys and subdued greens blend marvellously, and somehow you've caught the effect of the wind."

"Thank you. I'm pleased with it myself. But what's the matter, Carol? You look pale. Won't you sit down?"

She sat beside him on the log. "I'm all right. Mr Sullivan is conscious now and will be discharged soon. Mrs Ballins told me."

"Yes, I heard. It's good news."

She looked at his left arm, bandaged but no longer in a sling. "How's your wrist?"

"Still weak, but getting better. I thought at first that there must be a small bone broken, but it's only a bad sprain."

"It must have been difficult fixing the bolt on that gate up the quarry head. Wouldn't a chain have done?"

"I had a bolt. I didn't have a chain, and I was too lazy to go in and buy one. I didn't like to impose too much on Miss Tritt's offer to shop for us. I thought then it was pure kindness of heart." He laughed. "And if I have spare time myself I prefer to spend it painting, or talking to you."

"How fortunate it was your left wrist you hurt."

"Yes, it certainly was. Now tell me, what's upset you? You look as if you've had a fright."

Carol did not answer at once. She sat unmoving, staring out over the still grey waters of the lake. Then she spoke in a low voice. "More than a fright, John. A shock. I think I know why Josephine was killed."

"What?" He turned round towards her.

She did not look at him. She gazed over to the hills beyond the water as she went on, slowly, reflectively, as if talking to herself. "To kill in self-defence may be excusable. To kill from fear is just understandable. To kill for profit, or revenge, or hatred, is very wrong. But the reason for Josephine's murder was more wicked than any of that."

"What do you mean? What reason was there?"

She turned and faced him, looking directly into his eyes. "Josephine was not killed for gain. Nor from hatred, nor fear. She was killed with a cold, ruthless indifference. Her death was callously, casually carried out to fit into the composition of a picture. *To make the scene look natural.*"

"I don't understand."

"I have a theory. Would you care to hear it?"

"Of course. What's your theory, Carol?" He had put aside his painting materials and pad, and was giving her his full attention.

"Suppose — just suppose that you didn't fall down the quarry, John. Suppose you climbed down and rubbed a bit of skin off your forehead and held your wrist and lay there, calling for Mr Ballins, whom you knew to be working near by? Josephine came to see Susan and me the night before she died, and I've now remembered something she said. She told us that she had seen you on the slope the morning of your fall, and that she had thought at the time it was dangerous. But there is no slope on top of the quarry. It's a flat plateau. The slope up through the trees can't be called dangerous. So she could only have been referring to the shingle slope of the quarry itself. She saw you climbing down and considered it dangerous. It would look steeper from below than it actually is."

"This is most interesting. Do please go on." There was an acid tone in his voice.

"Josephine thought nothing of it. She probably assumed you had slipped while climbing on the slope. She said you told lies, but she was not referring to your supposed fall. We thought she meant you lied in saying she had talent, but it wasn't that either. As you say, you never praise falsely. I think she said it because she had seen you fixing a bolt on the gate — she told us so — and she knew you were lying about your wrist, because you were using both hands. One would *have* to use both hands to screw on a heavy eight-inch bolt. Josephine was an aloof girl, not interested in others' affairs. You were lying about your wrist. So what? That was your own business. She was a little puzzled and came to consult us about it, but she attached so little importance to it that after we'd talked for a bit on other matters she didn't even bother to tell us after all. It was not because of any suspicion or threats on her part that you pushed her over the bank."

"*I* pushed her over? What nonsense are you talking?"

Carol turned away from the intensity of his stare. She looked at the lake again as she went on, "You invited her to go up the hill with you to the quarry top, to show her how to render distance effects, which she told us all she found difficult. You are an outstanding teacher and she was eager for your advice. Mr Sullivan kept saying it was he who should have fallen that morning. He had difficulty with distance too, and he told us you had offered to go up with him and show him all you could. He was a good choice — small and frail. But he wouldn't come, so you persuaded Josephine instead. She was slight and thin. And anyone would do, anyone at all. It was all the same to you."

She turned to him again. He was

gazing at her, and his eyes — those eyes she had once thought so kind, so deep with warmth and understanding — those same eyes were cold, cruel, menacing. She felt a chill of fear and realised how rash she had been to speak as she had. But she forced herself to continue, trying to speak calmly while her heart was pounding and sweat beginning to form on her brow. "An accident to your wife alone would have brought you under suspicion. An accident to another person first would reduce the risk of suspicion, but one could still assume that one genuine accident had given you the idea of faking another. But an accident to yourself first, then to another, then to your wife — that was a better scheme, a nicely composed picture, which would 'look natural'. It didn't turn out as planned. Josephine's death was not considered an accident after all. Nor was your wife's. Murder was suspected. But you were quick to see how you could turn that to advantage.

Because although you might wish the death of your wife, no one could find a motive for your killing Josephine.

"Then I played into your hands by imagining that you, too, might have been pushed. What a good idea that seemed to you! How cleverly you suggested, by denial, that I was right. You were reluctant to accept the possibility, to accuse others. You said you had only the slight impression of a branch springing back on to your shoulders. How *could* a branch spring on to your back? If one is pushing through a thick scrub, branches can spring on to the face of someone behind, but not on to one's own back. You knew I'd realise that and be convinced it was a hand you felt, not a branch. I relayed my suspicions to others, as you hoped I would. I passed them on to the police, as you meant me to."

His eyes were on her, piercing, malevolent. But he did not speak. She must not betray her fear. She asked as coolly as she could, "Was your wife already up there, looking at the ground? Or did you persuade her to walk up with you, in your concern for the safety of the students?"

There was a silence which might have been thirty seconds, but which seemed interminable. Then he spoke evenly. "That is a very strange theory."

"It's more than a theory, isn't it? It's the truth."

"It's a theory which you should not repeat." He stroked his chin. "It would be most undesirable to have it repeated. No, don't get up." His left hand shot out and gripped her arm.

She sat still. He could not keep her down by holding one arm, but if she struggled he would rise, too, and she would be no match for him. Better to wait, to wait and watch for a moment when he relaxed his hold. Then she would pull away, spring up and run.

"Scream if you care to," he invited. "No one will hear you down here. And I assure you it is useless to struggle, if

314

you have that in mind. My arms are strong — both of them."

"So it's true, is it? I guessed correctly?"

"You guessed correctly. It was clever of you. But such a pity. I had become very fond of you, Carol. I had even hoped — no matter. You see my difficulty now, don't you?" He spoke gently, almost caressingly. "I *am* fond of you, but I really can't have you expounding your theory to others just when they're inclining to the idea of a wandering maniac."

"If you're proposing to drag *me* up to the quarry head you'll find your hands full. I'm a great deal stronger than Josephine or Mr Sullivan."

"No, I don't think I need go to those lengths. There's a dinghy on the lake. You haven't tried our dinghy yet? We may go for a row. In the meantime — I'm sorry, my dear. I'm truly sorry." His left hand tightened on her arm. With his right he began slowly undoing his scarf.

20

STEIN returned to the common-room looking rather despondent. "Come for a walk, Sue?"

"I think I'd better wait until Carol comes back. She suddenly got a bit upset and went outside. Vance thinks she's better left alone, but I'd like to be here when she gets back."

"What upset her?"

"We don't know. It was as though she'd just realised something or remembered something. She went off mumbling about a painting."

"The *construction* of a painting," said Myra. "Putting bits together to form it. Maybe she's solved our murders."

"Where did she go?" asked Stein.

"Outside," Susan told him. "Probably to find John Flavell. They're very friendly now, and if she had a problem she'd go to him, I think."

Stein's face hardened. "Vance, come with me, will you? We'd better find her."

"Why? Is anything wrong?"

They were already out of the door before Stein answered. "I hope not. But if she thinks she's on to something connected with the murders — she's an outspoken, imprudent young woman at times. Have you any idea where Flavell might be?"

"He has a commission for a painting of the lake. He could be there."

"We'll look. Come on." Stein walked quickly out the front door and round to the kitchen garden.

"What's the hurry?"

Stein was striding rapidly along the track.

"Nothing really." But he did not slacken his pace. "It's just that if Carol starts blurting out accusations — murder becomes progressively easier, you know. When a fellow thinks he's got away with a couple of killings he tends to lose reason, or caution. Any threat to his secret and he may strike quite rashly to remove it. I *don't* think there's any risk to Carol. He's under surveillance, but — "

"He? Who? What are you talking about?"

"Flavell. He's our killer. And if Carol has gone to —

"*Flavell*? And Carol's with him? Good God, man, what the hell are you dawdling for?" Vance raced madly ahead through the trees.

But when Rudolph caught up with him he was standing still. He pointed dumbly down the slope. Four figures were climbing up towards the house. Flavell was flanked by two burly plain-clothes men. Carol was a little way behind, stumbling unsteadily, slowly.

Then Vance ran down the hillside to meet her, ignoring the three men he passed. She fell against him. "Vance! He — I — It was — when he — "

"How strangely you express yourself,

Golliwog. You'll make a poet yet."

"Oh, blast it, I'm going to cry."

"Go right ahead, darling. I shall write an ode to your red eyes."

★ ★ ★

"You were never in any real danger," said Rudolph. "He was being watched. Lang had a couple of men in the trees, and as soon as you screamed they moved in."

They were sitting in the common-room, Myra, Vance, Stein, Carol and Susan. Mrs Ballins had produced a bottle of sherry, and Carol was beginning to relax.

"And if she hadn't had time to scream?" demanded Vance indignantly.

Rudolph conceded, "Oh well, that might have been a little awkward. But I don't think he would have *strangled* you," he told Carol consolingly. "He was more likely thinking of gagging you with that scarf while he thought of something else."

"He was going to take me out in the dinghy."

"Oh, I see. A drowning accident? Anyway, it was all very fortunate, because now Lang can take him in on a charge of assault."

"Of all the callous, unfeeling policemen — " began Vance.

Rudolph ignored him. "Lang suspected him from the first. It was just the tie-up with the girl's death that puzzled him."

"What made him suspect?" asked Susan.

"He was the only one to benefit from Mrs Flavell's death, and he had obviously lied about his fall."

"How did the inspector know that? He wasn't here then."

"No, but I was, and I'd seen the quarry. If a man rolls and bounces down a muddy gravelly slope like that, he doesn't have just one single patch of dirt on the back of his jacket. He'd have been wiser to change his clothes before he came into the studio."

"He always painted in that jacket," said Carol. "It was his favourite."

"He had obviously just climbed down and arranged himself on the ledge. It was also clear that he was lying about his wrist. He used that hand too often. He was conceited and careless and didn't always make sure he was alone when he used it. What was his reason for faking that fall? At the time it was puzzling, but unimportant. After the murders, it brought him under suspicion. He'd have done better to leave his own accident out of the picture he was constructing."

"Rot," said Myra. "He was planning accidents. Jolly good idea to have three. Artistically speaking, it was well thought out."

"Oh no," Stein objected. "One simple push to his wife would have been the thing. Suspicious, perhaps, but hard to prove him responsible. He always *did* put too much in his pictures. His one fault as a painter."

"I don't agree at all," said Myra.

"You tend to over-simplify. If he had — "

Susan broke in. "*Will* you two stop arguing? Rudy, was it Mr Flavell who jiggered up Mr Sullivan's car?"

"I imagine so. He knew the hand-brake was out of action and that Sullivan was going in to Little Dorley. It would be a matter of seconds to nick a hole in the brake-line or loosen the feeder valves. The garage fellows will have a report in shortly."

"Why did he do it? He didn't need any more accidents."

"Because what Sullivan was saying was so very alarmingly true. He *had* been the chosen victim. It should have been him. He was small and light, and willing to accompany Flavell up the hill to study distance effects. When he refused that morning, Flavell invited Josephine, who was always walking round at that hour."

"But that was no reason for trying to kill him later."

"No. But Mr Sullivan kept saying

it should have been him. He meant nothing more, he suspected nothing. But Flavell didn't know that. He thought the old fellow might have guessed. To a man with two murders to his credit, it was a threat. Then Sullivan announced he was going to tell the inspector about his qualms. It was just as well to remove him before he did. He failed, but it was a good try."

"Will they be able to prove it all? Will he be convicted?"

"He'll crack," said Stein. "His type always do."

There was a pause. Then Carol turned to Susan. "Sue, what about that premonition of yours the first night we arrived? Did you really foresee something like this?"

"Oh, *that*," said Susan, smiling. "I meant to tell you. I realised what that was. When I was four years old I got lost in Trafalgar Square. I guess the lions look enormous to a four-year-old. I remember how frightened I was that they would jump down and eat me before my mother found me. It must have been the sight of those stone cheetahs that brought back that awful fear."

"They're not a *bit* like lions," said Rudolph reprovingly. "I *showed* you the difference."

"Yes, I know, Rudy, but they looked just as hungry." She held out her glass for him to refill.

THE END

Other titles in the
Linford Mystery Library:

A GENTEEL LITTLE MURDER
Philip Daniels

Gilbert had a long-cherished plan to murder his wife. When the polished Edward entered the scene Gilbert's attitude was suddenly changed.

DEATH AT THE WEDDING
Madelaine Duke

Dr. Norah North's search for a killer takes her from a wedding to a private hospital.

MURDER FIRST CLASS
Ron Ellis

Will Detective Chief Inspector Glass find the Post Office robbers before the Executioner gets to them?

A FOOT IN THE GRAVE
Bruce Marshall

About to be imprisoned and tortured in Buenos Aires, John Smith escapes, only to become involved in an aeroplane hijacking.

DEAD TROUBLE
Martin Carroll

Trespassing brought Jennifer Denning more than she bargained for. She was totally unprepared for the violence which was to lie in her path.

HOURS TO KILL
Ursula Curtiss

Margaret went to New Mexico to look after her sick sister's rented house and felt a sharp edge of fear when the absent landlady arrived.

THE DEATH OF ABBE DIDIER
Richard Grayson

Inspector Gautier of the Sûreté investigates three crimes which are strangely connected.

NIGHTMARE TIME
Hugh Pentecost

Have the missing major and his wife met with foul play somewhere in the Beaumont Hotel, or is their disappearance a carefully planned step in an act of treason?

BLOOD WILL OUT
Margaret Carr

Why was the manor house so oddly familiar to Elinor Howard? Who would have guessed that a Sunday School outing could lead to murder?

THE DRACULA MURDERS
Philip Daniels

The Horror Ball was interrupted by a spectral figure who warned the merrymakers they were tampering with the unknown.

THE LADIES
OF LAMBTON GREEN
Liza Shepherd

Why did murdered Robin Colquhoun's picture pose such a threat to the ladies of Lambton Green?

CARNABY
AND THE GAOLBREAKERS
Peter N. Walker

Detective Sergeant James Aloysius Carnaby-King is sent to prison as bait. When he joins in an escape he is thrown headfirst into a vicious murder hunt.

MUD IN HIS EYE
Gerald Hammond

The harbourmaster's body is found mangled beneath Major Smyle's yacht. What is the sinister significance of the illicit oysters?

THE SCAVENGERS
Bill Knox

Among the masses of struggling fish in the *Tecta*'s nets was a larger, darker, ominously motionless form . . . the body of a skin diver.

DEATH IN ARCADY
Stella Phillips

Detective Inspector Matthew Furnival works unofficially with the local police when a brutal murder takes place in a caravan camp.

STORM CENTRE
Douglas Clark

Detective Chief Superintendent Masters, temporarily lecturing in a police staff college, finds there's more to the job than a few weeks relaxation in a rural setting.

THE MANUSCRIPT MURDERS
Roy Harley Lewis

Antiquarian bookseller Matthew Coll, acquires a rare 16th century manuscript. But when the Dutch professor who had discovered the journal is murdered, Coll begins to doubt its authenticity.

SHARENDEL
Margaret Carr

Ruth didn't want all that money. And she didn't want Aunt Cass to die. But at Sharendel things looked different. She began to wonder if she had a split personality.